SIDDHARTHA

SIDDHARTHA

Hermann Hesse

PILGRIMS PUBLISHING

◆ Varanasi ◆

SIDDHARTHA
Hermann Hesse

Published by:
PILGRIMS PUBLISHING

An imprint of:
PILGRIMS BOOK HOUSE
(Distributors in India)
B 27/98 A-8, Nawabganj Road
Durga Kund, Varanasi-221010, India
Tel: 91-542- 2314060,
Fax: 91-542- 2312456
E-mail: pilgrims@satyam.net.in
Website: www.pilgrimsbooks.com

Cover design by Asha

ISBN: 81-7769-573-8

Printed in India at Pilgrim Press Pvt. Ltd. Lalpur Varanasi

Preface to the New Edition

The story is set at the time of the teachings of Gautama, the earthly Buddha Sakyamuni. It is a torrid yarn of human suffering, of joy and romance. But its themes are much more complex, for here, within the beautifully written prose, is an in-depth analysis of Buddhism itself.

This is no ordinary story of the life of the Buddha, but a pleasing tale that follows the life of a 'lost soul', Siddhartha, living very much in parallel to the great Buddha, Gautama, himself. Herman Hesse has cleverly sought to question as well as explain some of the teachings that Buddhism suggests.

Our central character is seeking to expose the very essence of his soul, to find a path for human existence that is true and free of the baggage of normality. But can such a way be found?

In these pages we are confronted with every aspect of human life, and the picture is far from reassuring at times. And yet, despite even his abhorrence of teachers, including the Buddha Gautama, Siddhartha continues his search. It is a search that will take the reader through every layer of human endeavour, a heartrending story that will shake the foundations of any inquiring mind.

Bob Gibbons
Siân Pritchard-Jones

The Brahmin's Son

In the shade of the house, in the sunshine on the riverbank by the boats, in the shade of the sallow wood and the fig tree, Siddhartha, the handsome Brahmin's son grew with his friend Govinda. The sun browned his slender shoulders on the riverbank, while bathing at the holy ablutions, at the holy sacrifices. Shadows passed across his eyes in the mango grove during play, while his mother sang, during his father's teachings, when with the learned men. Siddhartha had already long taken part in the learned men's conversations, had engaged in debate with Govinda and had practised the art of contemplation and meditation with him. Already he knew how to pronounce Om silently—this word of words, to say it inwardly with the intake of breath, then breathing out with all his soul, his brow radiating the glow of pure spirit. Already he knew how to recognise Atman within the depths of his being, indestructible, at one with the universe.

There was happiness in his father's heart because of his son, who was intelligent and thirsty for knowledge; he saw him growing up to be a great, learned man, a priest, a prince among Brahmins.

There was pride in his mother's breast when she saw him walking, sitting down and rising: Siddhartha, strong, handsome, supple-limbed, greeting her with complete grace. Love stirred in the hearts of the young Brahmins' daughters when Siddhartha appeared, with his lofty brow, his king-like eyes and his slim figure.

Govinda, his friend, the Brahmin's son, loved him more than anybody else. He loved Siddhartha's eyes and clear voice. He loved the way he walked, his complete grace of movement; he loved everything that Siddhartha did and said, and above all he loved his intellect, his fine ardent thoughts, his strong will, his high vocation. Govinda knew that he would not become an ordinary

Brahmin, a lazy sacrificial official, an avaricious dealer in magic sayings, a conceited worthless orator, a wicked sly priest, or just a good stupid sheep amongst a large herd. No, and he, Govinda, did not want to become any of these, not a Brahmin like ten thousand others of their kind. He wanted to follow Siddhartha, the beloved, and the magnificent. And if he ever became a god, if he ever entered the All-Radiant, then Govinda wanted to follow him as his friend, his companion, his servant, his lance bearer, and his shadow.

That was how everybody loved Siddhartha. He delighted and made everybody happy.

But Siddhartha himself was not happy. Wandering along the rosy paths of the fig garden or sitting in contemplation in the bluish shade of the grove or washing his limbs in the daily bath of atonement; there was yet no joy. When offering sacrifices in the depths of the shady mango wood with complete grace of manner, beloved by all, a joy to all, there was yet no joy in his own heart. Dreams and restless thoughts came flowing to him from the river, from the twinkling stars at night, from the sun's melting rays. Dreams and a rest-lessness of the soul came to him, arising from the smoke of the sacrifices, ema-nating from the verses of the Rig-Veda, trickling through from the teachings of the old Brahmins.

Siddhartha had begun to feel the seeds of dis-content within him. He had begun to feel that the love of his father and mother, and also the love of his friend Govinda, would not always make him happy, give him peace, satisfy and suffice him. He had begun to suspect that his worthy father and his other teachers, the wise Brahmins, had already passed on to him the bulk and best of their wisdom; they had already poured the sum total of their knowledge into his waiting vessel. But the vessel was not full, his in-tellect was not satisfied, his soul was not at peace, and his heart was not still. The ablutions were good, but they were water; they did not wash sins away, they did not relieve the dis-tressed heart. The sacrifices and the supplication of the gods were excellent, but were they everything? Did the sac-rifices give happiness?

And what about the gods? Was it really Prajapati who had created the world? Was it not Atman, He alone, who had created it? Were not the gods' forms created like me and you, mortal, transient? Was it therefore good and right, was it a sensible and worthy act to offer sacrifices to the gods? To whom else should one offer sacrifices, to whom else should one pay honour, but to Him, Atman, the Only One? And where was Atman to be found, where did He dwell, where did his eternal heart beat, if not within the Self, in the innermost in the eternal, which each person carried within him? But where was this Self, this innermost? It was not flesh and bone, it was not thought or consciousness. That was what the wise men taught. Where, then, was it? To press towards the Self, towards Atman—was there another way that was worth seeking?

Nobody showed the way, nobody knew it, neither his father, nor the teachers and wise men nor the holy songs. The Brahmins and their holy books knew everything, everything; they had gone into everything—the creation of the world, the origin of speech, food, inhalation, exhalation, the arrangement of the senses, the acts of the gods. They knew a tremendous number of things—but was it worthwhile knowing all these things if they did not know the one important thing, the only important thing?

Many verses of the holy books, above all the Upani-shads of Sama-Veda spoke of this innermost thing. It is written: "Your soul is the whole world." It says that when a man is asleep, he penetrates his innermost and dwells in Atman. There was wonderful wisdom in these verses; all the knowledge of the sages was told here in enchanting language, pure as honey collected by the bees. No, this tremendous amount of knowledge, collected and preserved by successive generations of wise Brahmins could not be easily overlooked. But where were the Brahmins, the priests, the wise men, who were successful not only in having this most profound knowledge, but in experiencing it? Where were the initiated who, attaining Atman in sleep, could retain it in consciousness, in life, everywhere, in speech and in action?

Siddhartha knew many worthy Brahmins, above all his father; holy, learned, of the highest esteem. His father was worthy of admiration; his manner was quiet and noble. He lived a good life, his words were wise; fine and noble thoughts dwelt in his head, but even he who knew so much, did he live in bliss, was he at peace? Was he not also a seeker, insatiable? Did he not go continually to the holy springs with an insatiable thirst, to the sacrifices, to books, to the Brahmins' discourses? Why must he, the blameless one, wash away his sins and endeavour to cleanse himself anew each day? Was Atman then not within him? Was not then the source within his own heart? One must find the source within one's own Self, one must possess it. Everything else was seeking a detour, error.

These were Siddhartha's thoughts; this was his thirst, his sorrow. He often repeated to himself the words from one of the Chandogya-Upanishads. "In truth, the name of Brahman is Satya. Indeed, he who knows it enters the heavenly world each day." It often seemed near, the heavenly world, but never had he quite reached it, never had he quenched the final thirst. And among the wise men that he knew and whose teachings he enjoyed, there was not one who had entirely reached it, the heavenly world, not one who had completely quenched the eternal thirst.

"Govinda," said Siddhartha to his friend, "Govinda, come with me to the banyan tree. We will practice meditation."

They went to the banyan tree and sat down, twenty paces apart. As he sat down ready to pronounce the Om, Siddhartha softly recited the verse:

> "Om is the bow, the arrow is the soul,
> Brahman is the arrow's goal
> at which one aims unflinchingly."

When the customary time for the practice of meditation had passed, Govinda rose. It was now evening. It was time to perform the evening ablutions. He called Siddhartha by his name; he did not reply. Siddhartha sat absorbed, his eyes staring as if directed at a distant goal, the tip of his tongue showing a little between his teeth. He did not seem to be breathing. He sat thus, lost in meditation, thinking Om, his soul as the arrow directed at Brahman.

Some Samanas once passed through Siddhartha's town. Wandering ascetics, they were three thin worn-out men, neither old nor young, with dusty and bleeding shoulders, practically naked, scorched by the sun, solitary, strange and hostile; lean jackals in the world of men. Around them hovered an atmosphere of still passion, of devastating service, of unpitying self-denial.

In the evening, after the hour of contemplation, Siddhartha said to Govinda: "Tomorrow morning, my friend, Siddhartha is going to join the Samanas. He is going to become a Samana."

Govinda blanched as he heard these words and read the decision in his friend's determined face, undeviating as the released arrow from the bow. Govinda realised from the first glance at his friend's face that now it was beginning. Siddhartha was going his own way; his destiny was begin-ning to unfold itself, and with his destiny, his own. And he became as pale as a dried banana skin.

"Oh, Siddhartha," he cried, "will your father permit it?"

Siddhartha looked at him like one who had just awakened. As quick as lightning he read Govinda's soul, read the anxiety, the resignation.

"We will not waste words, Govinda," he said softly. "Tomorrow at daybreak I will begin the life of the Samanas. Let us not discuss it again."

Siddhartha went into the room where his father was sitting on a mat made of bast. He went up behind his father and remained standing there until his father felt his presence. "Is it you, Siddhartha?" the Brahmin asked. "Then speak what is in your mind."

Siddhartha said: "With your permission, Father, I have come to tell you that I wish to leave your house tomorrow and join the ascetics. I wish to become a Samana. I trust my father will not object."

The Brahmin was silent so long that the stars passed across the small window and changed their design before the silence in the room was finally broken. His son stood silent and motionless with his arms folded. The father, silent and motionless, sat on the mat, and the stars passed across the sky. Then his father said: "It is not seemly for Brahmins to utter forceful and angry words, but there is displeasure in my heart. I should not like to hear you make this request a second time."

The Brahmin rose slowly. Siddhartha remained silent with folded arms.

"Why are you waiting?" asked his father.

"You know why," answered Siddhartha.

His father left the room displeased and lay down on his bed.

As an hour passed by and he could not sleep, the Brahmin rose, wandered up and down and then left the house. He looked through the small window of the room and saw Siddhartha standing there with his arms folded, unmoving. He could see his pale robe shimmering. His heart troubled, the father returned to his bed.

As another hour passed and the Brahmin could not sleep, he rose again, walked up and down, left the house and saw the moon had risen.

He looked through the window. Siddhartha stood there unmoving, his arms folded; the moon shone on his bare shinbones. His heart troubled, the father went to bed.

He returned again after an hour and again after two hours, looked through the window and saw Siddhartha standing there in the moonlight, in the starlight, in the dark. And he came silently again, hour after hour, looked into the room, and saw him standing unmoving. His heart filled with anger, with anxiety, with fear, with sorrow.

And in the last hour of the night, before daybreak, he returned again, entered the room and saw the youth standing there. He seemed tall and a stranger to him.

"Siddhartha," he said, "why are you waiting?"

"You know why."

"Will you go on standing and waiting until it is day, noon, evening?"

"I will stand and wait."

"You will grow tired, Siddhartha."

"I will not grow tired."

"You will fall asleep, Siddhartha."

"I will not fall asleep."

"You will die, Siddhartha."

"I will not die."

"And would you rather die than obey your father?"

"Siddhartha has always obeyed his father."

"So you will give up your project?"

"Siddhartha will do what his father tells him."

The first light of day entered the room. The Brahmin saw that Siddhartha's knees trembled slightly, but there was no trembling in Siddhartha's face; his eyes looked faraway. Then the father realised that Siddhartha could no longer remain with him at home, that he had already left him.

The father touched Siddhartha's shoulder.

"You will go into the forest," he said, "and become a Samana. If you find bliss in the forest, come back and teach it to me. If you find disillusionment, come back, and we shall again offer sacrifices to the Gods together. Now go, kiss your mother, tell her where you are going. For me, however, it is the time to go to the river and perform the first ablution."

He dropped his hand from his son's shoulder and went out. Siddhartha swayed as he tried to walk. He controlled himself, bowed to his father and went to his mother to do what had been told to him.

As, with benumbed legs, he slowly left the still sleeping town at daybreak, a crouching shadow emerged from the last hut and joined the pilgrim. It was Govinda.

"You have come," said Siddhartha and smiled.

"I have come," said Govinda.

With the Samanas

On the evening of that day they overtook the Samanas and requested their company and allegiance. They were accepted.

Siddhartha gave his clothes to a poor Brahmin on the road and only retained his loincloth and earth-coloured, unstitched cloak. He only ate once a day and never cooked food. He fasted for fourteen days. He fasted for twenty-eight days. The flesh disappeared from his legs and cheeks. Strange dreams were reflected in his enlarged eyes. The nails grew long on his thin fingers and a dry, bristly beard appeared on his chin. His glance became icy when he encountered women; his lips curled with contempt when he passed through a town of well-dressed people. He saw businessmen trading, princes going to the hunt, mourners weeping over their dead and prostitutes offering themselves. He saw doctors attending the sick, priests deciding the day for sowing, lovers making love, mothers soothing their children—and all were not worth a passing glance, everything lied, stank of lies; they were all illusions of sense, happiness and beauty. All were doomed to decay. The world tasted bitter. Life was pain.

Siddhartha had one single goal—to become empty, to become empty of thirst, desire, dreams, pleasure and sorrow—to let the Self die. No longer to be Self, to experience the peace of an emptied heart, to experience pure thought, that was his goal. When all the Self was conquered and dead, when all passions and desires were silent, then the last must awaken, the innermost of being that is no longer Self—the great secret!

Silently Siddhartha stood in the fierce sun's rays, filled with pain and thirst, and stood until he no longer felt pain and thirst. Silently he stood in the rain, water dripping from his hair on to his freezing shoulders, on to his freezing hips and legs. And the ascetic stood until his shoulders and legs no longer froze, till they were silent, till they were still. Silently he crouched among the thorns. Blood dripped from his smarting skin, ulcers formed, and Siddhartha remained stiff, motionless, till no more blood flowed, till there was no more pricking, no more smarting.

Siddhartha sat upright and learned to save his breath, to manage with little breathing, to hold his breath. He learned, while breathing in, to quiet his heartbeat; he learned to lessen his heartbeats, until there were few and hardly any more.

Instructed by the eldest of the Samanas, Siddhartha practised self-denial and meditation according to the Samana's rules. A heron flew over the bamboo wood and Siddhartha took the heron into his soul, flew over forest and mountains, became a heron, ate fishes, suffered heron hunger, used heron language, and died a heron's death. A dead jackal lay on the sandy shore and Siddhartha's soul slipped into its corpse; he became a dead jackal, lay on the shore, swelled, stank, decayed and was dismembered by hyenas. He was picked at by vultures, became a skeleton, became dust and mingled with the atmosphere. And Siddhartha's soul returned, died, decayed, turned into dust; he experienced the troubled course of the life cycle. He waited with new thirst like a hunter at a chasm where the life cycle ends, where there is an end to causes, where painless eternity begins. He killed his senses, he killed his memory, he slipped out of his Self in a thousand different forms. He was animal, carcass, stone, wood, water, and each time he reawakened. The sun or moon shone, he was again Self, swung into the life cycle, felt thirst, conquered thirst, felt new thirst.

Siddhartha learned a great deal from the Samanas; he learned many ways of losing the Self. He travelled along the path of self-denial through pain, through voluntary suffering and conquering of pain, through hunger, thirst and fatigue. He travelled the way of self-denial through meditation, through the emptying of the mind of all images. Along these and other paths did he learn to travel. He lost his Self a thousand times, and for days on end he dwelt in non-being. But although the paths took him away from Self, in the end they always led back to it. Although Siddhartha fled from the Self a thousand times, he dwelt in nothing, he dwelt in animal and stone, the return was inevitable. The hour was inevitable when he would again find himself, in sun-shine or in moonlight, in shadow or in rain, and was again Self and Siddhartha, he again felt the torment of the onerous life cycle.

At his side lived Govinda, his shadow; he travelled along the same path, made the same endeavours. They rarely conversed with each other, apart from the necessities of their service and practices. Sometimes they went together through the villages in order to beg food for themselves and their teachers.

"What do you think, Govinda?" Siddhartha asked at the beginning of one of these expeditions. "Do you think we are any further? Have we reached our goal?"

Govinda replied: "We have learned and we are still learning. You will become a great Samana, Siddhartha. You have learned each exercise quickly.

The old Samanas have often appraised you. Some day you will be a holy man, Siddhartha."

Siddhartha said: "It does not appear so to me, my friend. What I have so far learned from the Samanas, I could have learned more quickly and easily in every inn in a prostitute's quarter, amongst the carriers and dice players."

Govinda said: "Siddhartha is joking. How could you have learned meditation, holding of the breath and insensibility towards hunger and pain, with those wretches?"

And Siddhartha said softly, as if speaking to himself: "What is meditation? What is abandonment of the body? What is fasting? What is the holding of breath? It is a flight from the Self, it is a temporary escape from the torment of Self. It is a temporary palliative against the pain and folly of life. The driver of oxen makes this same flight, takes this temporary drug when he drinks a few bowls of rice wine or coconut milk in the inn. He then no longer feels his Self, no longer feels the pain of life; he then experiences temporary escape. Falling asleep over his bowl of rice wine,

he finds what Siddhartha and Govinda find when
they escape from their bodies by long exercises
and dwelling in the non-Self."

Govinda said: "You speak thus, my friend,
and yet you know that Siddhartha is no driver of
oxen and a Samana is no drunkard. The drinker
does indeed find escape, he does indeed find a
short respite and rest, but he returns from the illusion and finds everything as it was before. He has
not grown wiser, he has not gained knowl-edge,
he has not climbed any higher."

Siddhartha answered with a smile on his face:
"I do not know. I have never been a drunkard.
But that I, Siddhartha, only find a short respite in
my exercises and meditation, and am as remote
from wisdom, from salvation, as a child in the
womb; that, Govinda, I do know."

On another occasion when Siddhartha left the
wood with Govinda in order to beg for food for
their brothers and teachers, Siddhartha began to
speak and said: "Well, Govinda, are we on the
right road? Are we gaining knowledge? Are we
approaching salvation? Or are we perhaps going

in circles, we who thought to escape from the cycle?"

Govinda said: "We have learned much, Siddhartha. There still remains much to learn. We are not going in circles; we are going upwards. The path is a spiral; we have already climbed many steps."

Siddhartha replied: "How old, do you think, is our oldest Samana, our worthy teacher?"

Govinda said: "I think the eldest would be about sixty years old."

And Siddhartha said: "He is sixty years old and has not attained Nirvana. He will be seventy and eighty years old, and you and I, we shall grow as old as he, and do exercises and fast and meditate, but we will not attain Nirvana, neither he nor we. Govinda, I believe that amongst all the Samanas, probably not even one will attain Nirvana. We find consolations, we learn tricks with which we deceive ourselves, but the essential thing—the way—we do not find."

"Do not utter such dreadful words, Siddhartha," said Govinda. "How could it be that amongst so many learned men, amongst so many Brahmins, amongst so many austere and worthy Samanas, amongst so many seekers, so many devoted to the inner life, so many holy men, none will find the right way?"

Siddhartha, however, said in a voice, which contained as much grief as mockery, in a soft, somewhat sad, somewhat jesting voice: "Soon, Govinda, your friend will leave the path of the Samanas along which he has travelled with you so long. I suffer thirst, Govinda, and on this long Samana path my thirst has not grown less. I have always thirsted for knowledge; I have always been full of questions. Year after year I have questioned the Brahmins. Year after year I have questioned the holy Vedas. Perhaps, Govinda, it would have been equally good, equally clever and holy if I had questioned the rhinoceros or the chimpanzee. I have spent a long time and have not yet finished, in order to learn this, Govinda: that one can learn nothing. There is, so I believe, in the essence of everything, something that we cannot call learning. There is, my friend, only a knowledge—that is everywhere, that is Atman, that is in me and you and in every creature, and I am beginning to believe that this knowledge has no worse enemy than the man of knowledge, than learning."

Thereupon Govinda stood still on the path, raised his hands and said: "Siddhartha, do not distress your friend with such talk. Truly, your words trouble me. Think, what meaning would our holy prayers have, the veneration of the Brahmins, the holiness of the Samanas, if, as you say, there is no learning? Siddhartha, what would become of everything, what would be holy on earth, what would be precious and sacred?"

Govinda murmured a verse to himself, a verse from one of the Upanishads:

"He whose reflective pure spirit sinks into Atman
Knows bliss inexpressible through words."

Siddhartha was silent. He dwelt long on the words which Govinda had uttered.

Yes, he thought, standing with bowed head, what remains from all that seems holy to us? What remains? What is preserved? And he shook his head.

Once, when both youths had lived with the Samanas for about three years and shared their practices, they heard from many sources a rumour, a report. Someone had appeared, called Gautama, the Illustrious, the Buddha. He had conquered in himself the sorrows of the world and had brought to a standstill the cycle of rebirth. He wandered through the country preaching, surrounded by disciples, having no possessions, homeless, without a wife, wearing the yellow cloak of an ascetic, but with a lofty brow, a holy man; Brahmins and princes bowed before him and became his pupils.

This report, this rumour, this tale was heard and spread here and there. The Brahmins talked about it in the town, the Samanas in the forest. The name of Gautama, the Buddha, continually reached the ears of the young men, spoken of well and ill, in praise and in scorn.

Just as when a country is ravaged with the plague and a rumour arises that there is a man, a wise man, a learned man, whose words and breath are sufficient to heal the afflicted, and as the report travels across the country and everyone speaks about it, many believe and many doubt it. Many, however, immediately go on their way to seek the wise man, the benefactor. In such a manner did that rumour, that happy report of Gautama, the Buddha, the wise man from the race of Sakya, travel through the country. He possessed great knowledge, said the believers; he remembered his former lives, he had attained Nirvana and never returned to the cycle, he plunged no more into the troubled stream of forms. Many wonderful and incredible things were reported about him; he had performed wonders, had conquered the devil, and had spoken with the gods. His enemies and doubters, however, said that this Gautama was an idle fraud; he passed his days in high living, scorned sacrifices, was unlearned and knew neither practices nor mortification of the flesh.

The rumours of the Buddha sounded attractive; there was magic in these reports. The world was sick, life was difficult and here there seemed new hope, here there seemed to be a message, comforting, mild, full of fine promises. Everywhere there were rumours about the Buddha. Young men all over India listened, felt a longing and a hope. And among the Brahmins' sons in the towns and villages, every pilgrim and stranger was welcome if he brought news of him, the Illustrious, the Sakyamuni.

The rumours reached the Samanas in the forest and Siddhartha and Govinda, a little at a time, every little item heavy with hope, heavy with doubt. They spoke little about it, as the eldest Samana was no friend of this rumour. He had heard that this alleged Buddha had formerly been an ascetic and had lived in the woods, but had then turned to high living and the pleasures of the world, and he held no brief for this Gautama.

"Siddhartha," Govinda once said to his friend, "today I was in the village and a Brahmin invited

me to enter his house and in the house was a
Brahmin's son from Magadha; he had seen the
Buddha with his own eyes and had heard him
preach. Truly I was filled with longing; and I
thought, I wish that both Siddhartha and I might
live to see the day when we can hear the teachings from the lips of the Perfect One. My friend,
shall we not also go hither and hear the teachings
from the lips of the Buddha?"

Siddhartha said: "I always thought that
Govinda would remain with the Samanas. I always believed it was his goal to be sixty and seventy years old and still practice the arts and exercises that the Samanas teach. But how little did I
know Govinda! How little did I know what was
in his heart! Now, my dear friend, you wish to
strike a new path and go to hear the Buddha's
teachings."

Govinda said: "It gives you pleasure to mock
me. No matter if you do, Siddhartha. Do you not
also feel a longing, a desire to hear this teaching?
And did you not once say to me, I will not travel
the path of the Samanas much longer?"

Then Siddhartha laughed in such a way that his voice expressed a shade of sorrow and a shade of mockery. He said: "You have spoken well, Govinda, you have remembered well, but you must also remember what else I told you, that I have become distrustful of teachings and learning and that I have little faith in words that come to us from teachers. But, very well, my friend, I am ready to hear that new teaching, although I believe in my heart that we have already tasted the best fruit of it."

Govinda replied: "I am delighted that you are agreed. But tell me, how can the teachings of Gautama disclose to us their most precious fruit before we have even heard him?"

Siddhartha said: "Let us enjoy this fruit and await further ones, Govinda. This fruit, for which we are already indebted to Gautama, consists of the fact that he has enticed us away from the Samanas. Whether there are still other and better fruits, let us patiently wait and see."

On the same day, Siddhartha informed the eldest Samana of his decision to leave him. He told

the old man with the politeness and modesty fitting
to young men and students. But the old man was
angry that both young men wished to leave him
and he raised his voice and scolded them strongly.

Govinda was taken aback, but Siddhartha put
his lips to Govinda's ear and whispered: "Now I
will show the old man that I have learned something from him."

He stood near the Samana, his mind intent; he
looked into the old man's eyes and held him with
his look, hypnotised him, made him mute, conquered his will, commanded him silently to do as
he wished. The old man became silent, his eyes
glazed, his will crippled; his arms hung down, he
was powerless under Siddhartha's spell.
Siddhartha's thoughts conquered those of the
Samana; he had to perform what they commanded.
And so the old man bowed several times; gave his
blessings and stammered his wishes for a good
journey. The young men thanked him for his good
wishes, returned his bow, and departed.

On the way, Govinda said: "Siddhartha, you
have learned more from the Samanas than I was

aware of. It is difficult, very difficult to hypnotise an old Samana. In truth, if you had stayed there, you would have soon learned how to walk on water."

"I have no desire to walk on water," said Siddhartha. "Let the old Samanas satisfy themselves with such arts."

Gautama

In the town of Savathi every child knew the name of the illustrious Buddha and every house was ready to fill the alms bowls of Gautama's silently begging disciples. Near the town was Gautama's favourite abode, the Jetavana grove, which the rich merchant Anathapindika, a great devotee of the Illustrious One, had presented to him and his followers.

The two young ascetics, in their search for Gautama's abode, had been referred to this district by tales and answers to their questions, and on their arrival in Savathi, food was offered to them immediately at the first house in front of whose door they stood silently begging. They partook of food and Siddhartha asked the lady who handed him the food: "Good lady, we should very much like to know where the Buddha, the Illustrious One, dwells. We are two Samanas from the forest and have come to see the Perfect One and hear his teachings from his own lips."

The woman said: "You have come to the right place, O Samanas from the forest. The Illustrious One sojourns in Jetavana, in the garden of Anathapindika. You may spend the night there, pilgrims, for there is enough room for the numerous people who flock here to hear the teachings from his lips."

Then Govinda rejoiced and happily said: "Ah, then we have reached our goal and our journey is at an end. But tell us, mother of pilgrims, do you know the Buddha? Have you seen him with your own eyes?"

The woman said: "I have seen the Illustrious One many times. On many a day I have seen him walk through the streets, silently, in a yellow cloak, and silently hold out his alms bowl at the house doors and return with his filled bowl."

Govinda listened, enchanted, and wanted to ask many more questions and hear much more, but Siddhartha reminded him that it was time to go. They expressed their thanks and departed. It was hardly necessary to enquire the way, for quite a number of pilgrims and monks from Gautama's followers were on the way to Jetavana. When they arrived there at night, there were continually new arrivals. There was a stir of voices from them, requesting and obtaining shelter. The two Samanas, who were used to life in the forest, quickly and quietly found shelter and stayed there till morning.

At sunrise they were astounded to see the large num-ber of believers and curious people who had spent the night there. Monks in yellow robes wandered along all the paths of the magnificent grove. Here and there they sat under the trees, lost in meditation or engaged in spirited talk. The shady gardens were like a town, swarming with bees. Most of the monks departed with their alms bowls, in order to obtain food for their midday meal, the only one of the day. Even the Buddha himself went begging in the morning.

Siddhartha saw him and recognised him immediately, as if pointed out to him by a god. He saw him, bearing an alms bowl, quietly leaving the place, an unassuming man in a yellow cowl.

"Look," said Siddhartha softly to Govinda, "there is the Buddha."

Govinda looked attentively at the monk in the yellow cowl, who could not be distinguished in any way from the hundreds of other monks, and yet Govinda soon recognised him. Yes, it was he, and they followed him and watched him.

The Buddha went quietly on his way, lost in thought. His peaceful countenance was neither happy nor sad. He seemed to be smiling gently inwardly. With a secret smile, not unlike that of a healthy child, he walked along, peacefully, quietly. He wore his gown and walked along exactly like the other monks. But his face and his step, his peaceful downward glance, his peaceful downward hanging hand, and every finger of his hand spoke of peace, spoke of completeness, sought nothing, imitated nothing, reflected a continuous quiet, an unfailing light, an invulnerable peace.

And so Gautama wandered into the town to obtain alms, and the two Samanas recognised him only by his complete peacefulness of demeanour, by the stillness of his form, in which there was no seeking, no will, no counterfeit, no effort, only light and peace.

"Today we will hear the teachings from his own lips," said Govinda.

Siddhartha did not reply. He was not very curious about the teachings. He did not think they would teach him anything new. He, as well as Govinda, had heard the substance of the Buddha's teachings, if only from second and third-hand reports. But he looked attentively at Gautama's head, at his shoulders, at his feet, at his still, downward hanging hand, and it seemed to him that in every joint of every finger of his hand there was knowledge; they spoke, breathed, and radiated truth. This man, this Buddha, was truly a holy man to his fingertips. Never had Siddhartha esteemed a man so much, never had he loved a man so much.

They both followed the Buddha into the town and returned in silence. They themselves intended to abstain from food that day. They saw Gautama return, saw him take his meal within the circle of his disciples. What he ate would not have satisfied a bird and they saw him withdraw to the shade of the mango tree.

In the evening, however, when the heat abated and everyone in the camp was alert and gathered together, they heard the Buddha preach. They heard his voice, and this also was perfect, quiet and full of peace. Gautama talked about suffering, the origin of suffering, the way to release from suffering. Life was pain, the world was full of suffering, but the path to the release from suffering had been found. There was salvation for those who went the way of the Buddha.

The Illustrious One spoke in a soft but firm voice, he taught the four main points and taught the Eight-fold Paths; patiently he covered the usual method of teaching with examples and repetition. Clearly and quietly his voice was carried to his listeners, like a star in the heavens.

When the Buddha had finished it was already night; many pilgrims came forward and asked to be accepted into the community. The Buddha accepted them and said: "You have listened well to the teachings. Join us then and walk in bliss; put an end to suffering."

Govinda, the shy one, also stepped forward and said: "I also wish to pay my allegiance to the Illustrious One and his teachings." He asked to be taken into the community and was accepted.

As soon as the Buddha had withdrawn for the night, Govinda turned to Siddhartha and said eagerly: "Siddhartha, it is not for me to reproach you. We have both listened to the Illustrious One, we have both heard his teachings. Govinda has listened to the teachings and has accepted them, but you, my dear friend, will you not also tread the path of salvation? Will you delay, will you still wait?"

When he heard Govinda's words, Siddhartha awakened as if from a sleep. He looked at Govinda's face for a long time. Then he spoke softly and there was no mockery in his voice.

"Govinda, my friend, you have taken the step, you have chosen your path. You have always been my friend, Govinda, you have always gone a step behind me. Often I have thought, will Govinda ever take a step without me from his own convictions? Now, you are a man and have chosen your own path. May you go along it to the end, my friend. May you find salvation!"

Govinda, who did not yet fully understand, repeated his question impatiently: "Speak, my dear friend, say that you also cannot do other than swear allegiance to the Buddha."

Siddhartha placed his hand on Govinda's shoulder. "You have heard my blessing, Govinda. I repeat it. May you travel this path to the end. May you find salvation!"

In that moment, Govinda realised that his friend was leaving him and he began to weep.

"Siddhartha," he cried.

Siddhartha spoke kindly to him. "Do not forget, Govinda, that you now belong to the Buddha's holy men. You have renounced home and parents, you have renounced origin and property, you have renounced your own will, and you have renounced friendship. That is what the teachings preach, that is the will of the Illustrious One. That is what you wished yourself. Tomorrow, Govinda, I will leave you."

For a long time the friends wandered through the woods. They lay down for a long time but could not sleep. Govinda pressed his friend again and again to tell him why he would not follow the Buddha's teachings, what flaw he found in them, but each time Siddhartha waved him off: "Be at peace, Govinda. The Illustrious One's teachings are very good. How could I find a flaw in them?"

Early in the morning, one of the Buddha's followers, one of his oldest monks, went through the garden and called to him all the new people. Those who had sworn their allegiance to the teachings, in order to place upon them the yellow robe and instruct them in the first teachings and duties of their order. Thereupon Govinda tore himself away, embraced the friend of his youth, and drew on the monk's robe.

Siddhartha wandered through the grove deep in thought.

There he met Gautama, the Illustrious One, and as he greeted him respectfully and the Buddha's expression was so full of goodness and peace, the young man plucked up courage and asked the Illustrious One's permission to speak to him. Silently the Illustrious One nodded his permission.

Siddhartha said: "Yesterday, Oh Illustrious One, I had the pleasure of hearing your wonderful teachings. I came from afar with my friend to hear you, and now my friend will remain with you; he has sworn allegiance to you. I, however, am continuing my pilgrimage anew."

"As you wish," said the Illustrious One politely. "My talk is perhaps too bold," continued Siddhartha, "but I do not wish to leave the Illustrious One without sincerely communicating to him my thoughts. Will the Illustrious One hear me a little longer?"

Silently the Buddha nodded his consent.

Siddhartha said: "Oh Illustrious One, in one thing above all have I admired your teachings. Everything is completely clear and proved. You show the world as a complete, unbroken chain, an eternal chain, linked together by cause and effect. Never has it been presented so clearly, never has it been so irrefutably demonstrated. Surely every Brahmin's heart must beat more quickly, when through your teachings he looks at the world, com-pletely coherent, without a loophole, clear as crystal, not dependent on chance, not dependent on the gods. Whether it is good or evil, whether life in itself is pain or pleasure, whether it is uncertain—that it may perhaps be this is not important. But the unity of the world, the co-herence of all events, the embracing of the big and the small from the same stream, from the same law of cause, of becoming and dying; this shines clearly from your exalted teachings, O Perfect One.

"But according to your teachings, this unity and logical consequence of all things is broken in one place. Through a small gap there streams into the world of unity something strange, something

new, something that was not there before and that
cannot be demonstrated and proved; that is your
doctrine of rising above the world, of salvation.
Through this small break, however, the eternal
and single world law breaks down again. Forgive
me if I raise this objection."

Gautama had listened quietly, motionless. And
now the Perfect One spoke in his kind, polite and
clear voice. "You have listened well to the teachings, O Brahmin's son, and it is a credit to you
that you have thought so deeply about them. You
have found a flaw. Think well about it again. Let
me warn you, you who are thirsty for knowledge,
against the thicket of opinions and the conflict of
words. Opinions mean nothing; they may be beautiful or ugly, clever or foolish, anyone can embrace or reject them. The teaching, which you
have heard, however, is not my opinion, and its
goal is not to explain the world to those who are
thirsty for knowledge. Its goal is quite different;
its goal is salvation from suffering. That is what
Gautama teaches, nothing else."

"Do not be angry with me, O Illustrious One," said the young man. "I have not spoken to you thus to quarrel with you about words. You are right when you say that opinions mean little, but may I say one thing more. I did not doubt you for one moment. I did not doubt that you were the Buddha, that you have reached the highest goal which so many thousands of Brahmins and Brahmins' sons are striving to reach. You have done so by your own seeking, in your own way, through thought, through meditation, through knowledge, through enlightenment. You have learned nothing through teachings, and so I think, O Illustrious One, that nobody finds salvation through teachings. To nobody, O Illustrious One, can you communicate in words and teachings what happened to you in the hour of your enlightenment.

"The teachings of the enlightened Buddha embrace much, they teach much, how to live righteously, how to avoid evil. But there is one thing that this clear, worthy instruction does not contain; it does not contain the secret of what the Illustrious One himself experienced, he alone among hundreds of thousands. That is what I thought and realised when I heard your teachings. That is why I am going on my way, not to seek another and better doctrine, for I know there is none, but to leave all doctrines and all teachers and to reach my goal alone or die. But I will often remember this day, O Illustrious One, and this hour when my eyes beheld a holy man."

The Buddha's eyes were lowered, his unfathomable face expressed complete equanimity.

"I hope you are not mistaken in your reasoning," said the Illustrious One slowly. "May you reach your goal! But tell me, have you seen my gathering of holy men, my many brothers who have sworn allegiance to the teachings? Do you think, O Samana from afar, that it would be better for all these to relinquish the teachings and to return to the life of the world and desires?"

"That thought never occurred to me," cried Siddhartha. "May they all follow the teachings! May they reach their goal! It is not for me to judge another life. I must judge for myself. I must choose and reject. We Samanas seek release from the Self,

O Illustrious One. If I were one of your followers, I fear that it would only be on the surface. I would deceive myself that I was at peace and had attained salvation, while in truth the Self would continue to live and grow, for it would have been transformed into your teachings, into my allegiance and love for you and for the community of the monks."

Half smiling, with imperturbable brightness and friendliness, the Buddha looked steadily at the stranger and dismissed him with a hardly visible gesture.

"You are clever, O Samana," said the Illustrious One, "you know how to speak cleverly, my friend. Be on your guard against too much cleverness."

The Buddha walked away and his look and half-smile remained imprinted on Siddhartha's memory forever.

I have never seen a man look and smile, sit and walk like that, he thought. I, also, would like to look and smile, sit and walk like that, so free, so worthy, so restrained, so candid, so childlike and mysterious. A man only looks and walks like that when he has conquered his Self. I also will conquer my Self.

I have seen one man, one man only, thought Siddhartha, before whom I must lower my eyes. I will never lower my eyes before any other man. No other teachings will attract me, since this man's teachings have not done so.

The Buddha has robbed me, thought Siddhartha. He has robbed me, yet he has given me something of greater value. He has robbed me of my friend, who believed in me and who now believes in him; he was my shadow and is now in Gautama's shadow. But he has given to me Siddhartha, myself.

Awakening

As Siddhartha left the grove in which the Buddha, the Perfect One, and Govinda remained, he felt that he had also left his former life behind him in the grove. As he slowly went on his way, his head was full of this thought. He reflected deeply, until this feeling completely overwhelmed him and he reached a point where he recognised causes; for to recognise causes, it seemed to him, is to think, and through thought alone, feelings become knowledge and are not lost, but become real and begin to mature.

Siddhartha reflected deeply as he went on his way. He realised that he was no longer a youth; he was now a man. He realised that something had left him, like the old skin that a snake sheds. Something was no longer in him, something that had accompanied him right through his youth and was part of him; this was the desire to have teachers and to listen to their teachings. He had left the last teacher he had met, even he, the greatest and wisest teacher, the holiest, the Buddha. He had to leave him; he could not accept his teachings.

Slowly the thinker went on his way and asked himself: what is it that you wanted to learn from teachings and teachers, and although they taught you much, what was it they could not teach you? And he thought, it was the Self, the character and nature of which I wished to learn. I wanted to rid myself of the Self, to conquer it, but I could not conquer it, I could only deceive it. I could only fly from it, could only hide from it. Truly, nothing in the world has occupied my thoughts as much as the Self, this riddle, that I live, that I am one and am separated and different from everybody else, that I am Siddhartha; and about nothing in the world do I know less than about myself, about Siddhartha.

The thinker, slowly going on his way, suddenly stood still, gripped by this thought and another thought immediately arose from this one. It was: the reason why I do not know anything about myself, the reason why Siddhartha has remained alien and unknown to myself is due to one thing, to one single thing—I was afraid of myself, I was fleeing from myself. I was seeking Brahman, Atman, I wished to destroy myself, to get away from myself, in order to find in the unknown innermost, the nucleus of all things, Atman, Life, the Divine, the Absolute. But by doing so, I lost myself on the way.

Siddhartha looked up and around him, a smile crept over his face, and a strong feeling of awakening from a long dream spread right through his being. Immediately he walked on again, quickly, like a man who knows what he has to do.

Yes, he thought, breathing deeply, I will no longer try to escape from Siddhartha. I will no longer devote my thoughts to Atman and the sorrows of the world. I will no longer mutilate and destroy myself in order to find a secret behind the ruins. I will no longer study Yoga-Veda, Atharva-Veda, or asceticism, or any other teachings. I will learn from myself, be my own pupil; I will learn from myself the secret of Siddhartha.

He looked around him as if seeing the world for the first time. The world was beautiful, strange and mysterious. Here was blue, here was yellow, here was green, sky and river, woods and mountains, all beautiful, all mysterious and enchanting. And in the midst of it, he, Siddhartha, the awakened one, was on the way to himself. All this, all this yellow and blue, river and wood, passed for the first time across Siddhartha's eyes. It was no longer the magic of Mara, it was no more the veil of Maya, it was no longer meaningless and the chance diversities of the appearances of the world, despised by deep thinking Brahmins, who scorned diversity, who sought unity.

River was river, and if the One and Divine in Siddhartha secretly lived in blue and river, it was just the divine art and intention that there should be yellow and blue, there sky and wood—and here Siddhartha. Meaning and reality were not hidden somewhere behind things; they were in them, in all of them.

How deaf and stupid I have been, he thought, walking on quickly. When anyone reads anything which he wishes to study, he does not despise the letters and punctuation marks, and call them illusion, chance and worthless shells, but he reads them, he studies and loves them, letter by letter. But I, who wished to read the book of the world and the book of my own nature, did presume to despise the letters and signs. I called the world of appearances, illusion. I called my eyes and tongue, chance. Now it is over; I have awakened. I have indeed awakened and have only been born today.

But as these thoughts passed through Siddhartha's mind, he suddenly stood still, as if a snake lay in his path.

Then suddenly this also was clear to him: he, who was in fact like one who had awakened or was newly born, must begin his life completely afresh. When he left the Jetavana grove that morning, the grove of the Illustrious One, already awakened, already on the way to himself, it was his intention, and it seemed the natural course for him after the years of his asceticism, to return to his home and his father. Now, however, in that moment as he stood still, as if a snake lay in his path, this thought also came to him: I am no longer what I was, I am no longer an ascetic, no longer a priest, no longer a Brahmin. What then shall I do at home with my father? Study? Offer sacrifices? Practice meditation? All this is over for me now.

Siddhartha stood still and for a moment an icy chill stole over him. He shivered inwardly like a small animal, like a bird or a hare, when he realised how alone he was. He had been homeless for years and had not felt like this. Now he did feel it. Previously, when in deepest meditation, he was still his father's son, he was a Brahmin of high standing, a religious man. Now he was only Siddhartha, the awakened; otherwise nothing else. He breathed in deeply and for a moment he shuddered. Nobody was so alone as he. He was no nobleman, belonging to any aristocracy, no artisan belonging to any guild and finding refuge in it, sharing its life and language. He was no Brahmin, sharing the life of the Brahmins, no ascetic belonging to the Samanas. Even the most secluded hermit in the woods was not one and alone; he also belonged to a class of people. Govinda had become a monk and thousands of monks were his brothers, wore the same gown, shared his beliefs and spoke his language. But he, Siddhartha, where did he belong? Whose life would he share? Whose language would he speak?

At that moment, when the world around him melted away, when he stood alone like a star in the heavens, he was overwhelmed by a feeling of icy despair, but he was more firmly himself than ever. That was the last shudder of his awakening, the last pains of birth. Immediately he moved on again and began to walk quickly and impatiently, no longer homewards, no longer to his father, no longer looking backwards.

PART TWO

Kamala

Siddhartha learned something new on every step
of his path, for the world was transformed and he
was en-thralled. He saw the sun rise over forest
and mountains and set over the distant palm shore.
At night he saw the stars in the heavens and the
sickle-shaped moon floating like a boat in the blue.
He saw trees, stars, animals, clouds, rainbows,
rocks, weeds, flowers, brook and river, the sparkle
of dew on bushes in the morning, distant high
mountains blue and pale; birds sang, bees
hummed, the wind blew gently across the rice
fields. All this colour, and in a thousand different
forms, had always been there. The sun and moon
had always shone; the rivers had always flowed
and the bees had hummed. In previous times all

this had been nothing to Siddhartha but a fleeting and illusive veil before his eyes, regarded with distrust, condemned to be disregarded and ostracised from his thoughts, because it was not reality, because reality lay on the other side of the visible. But now his eyes lingered on this side; he saw and recognised the visible and he sought his place in this world.

He did not seek reality; his goal was not on any other side. The world was beautiful when looked at in this way, without any seeking, so simple, so childlike. The moon and the stars were beautiful, the brook, the shore, the forest and rock, the goat and the golden beetle, the flower and butterfly were beautiful. It was beautiful and pleasant to go through the world like that, so childlike, so awakened, so concerned with the immediate, without any distrust. Elsewhere, the sun burned fiercely; elsewhere there was cool in the forest shade; elsewhere there were pumpkins and bananas. The days and nights were short, every hour passed quickly like a sail on the sea, beneath the

sail of a ship full of treasures, full of joy. Siddhartha
saw a group of monkeys in the depths of the forest, moving about high in the branches, and heard
their wild eager cries. Siddhartha saw a ram follow a sheep and mate. In a lake of rushes he saw
a pike making chase in evening hunger. Swarms
of young fishes, fluttering and glistening, moved
anxiously away from it. Strength and desire were
reflected in the swiftly moving whirls of water
formed by the raging pursuer.

All this had always been and he had never
seen it; he was never present. Now he was present
and belonged to it. Through his eyes he saw light
and shadows; through his mind he was aware of
the moon and stars.

On the way, Siddhartha remembered all that
he had experienced in the garden of Jetavana, the
teachings that he had heard there from the holy
Buddha, the parting from Govinda and the conversation with the Illustrious One. He remembered
each word that he had said to the Illustrious One,
and he was astonished that he had said things which

he did not then really know. What he had said to
the Buddha, that the Buddha's wisdom and secret was not teachable, that it was inexpressible
and incommunicable and which he had once experienced in an hour of enlightenment, was just
what he had now set off to experience, what he
was now beginning to experience. He must gain
experience himself.

He had known for a long time that his Self
was Atman, of the same eternal nature as Brahman, but he had never really found his Self, because he had wanted to trap it in the net of
thoughts. The body was certainly not the Self,
nor the play of senses, nor thought, nor understanding, nor acquired wisdom nor art with which
to draw conclusions, nor from already existing
thoughts to spin new thoughts. No, this world of
thought was still on this side, and it led to no goal
when one destroyed the senses of the incidental
Self but fed it with thoughts and erudition. Both
thought and senses were fine things; behind
both of them lay hidden the last meaning. It was

worthwhile listening to them both, to play with both, neither to despise nor overrate either of them, but to listen intently to both voices.

He would only strive after whatever the inward voice commanded him, not tarry anywhere but where the voice advised him. Why did Gautama once sit down beneath the Bo tree in his greatest hour when he received enlightenment? He had heard a voice, a voice in his own heart which commanded him to seek rest under this tree, and he had not taken recourse to mortification of the flesh, sacrifices, bathing or prayers, eating or drinking, sleeping or dreaming; he had listened to the voice. To obey no other external command, only the voice, to be prepared, that was good, that was necessary. Nothing else was necessary.

During the night, as he slept in a ferryman's straw hut, Siddhartha had a dream. He dreamt that Govinda stood before him, in the yellow robe of the ascetic. Govinda looked sad and asked him, "Why did you leave me?" Thereupon he embraced Govinda, put his arm round him, and as he drew him to his breast and kissed him, he was Govinda no longer, but a woman. And out of the woman's gown emerged a full breast, and Siddhartha lay there and drank; sweet and strong tasting the milk from this breast. It tasted of woman and man, of sun and forest, of animal and flower, of every fruit, of every pleasure. It was intoxicating. When Siddhartha awoke, the pale river shimmered past the door of the hut, and in the forest the cry of an owl rang out, deep and clear.

As the day began, Siddhartha asked his host, the ferryman, to take him across the river. The ferryman took him across on his bamboo raft. The broad sheet of water glimmered pink in the light of the morning.

"It is a beautiful river," he said to his companion.

Yes," said the ferryman, "it is a very beautiful river. I love it above everything. I have often listened to it, gazed at it, and I have always learned something from it. One can learn much from a river."

"Thank you, good man," said Siddhartha, as he landed on the other side. "I am afraid I have no gift to give you, nor any payment. I am homeless, a Brahmin's son and Samana."

I could see that," said the ferryman, "and I did not expect any payment or gift from you. You will give it to me some other time."

"Do you think so?" asked Siddhartha merrily.

"Certainly. I have learned that from the river too; everything comes back. You, too, Samana, will come back. Now farewell, may your friendship be my payment! May you think of me when you sacrifice to the gods!"

Smiling, they parted from each other. Siddhartha was pleased at the ferryman's friendliness. He is like Govinda, he thought, smiling. All whom I meet on the way are like Govinda. All are grateful, although they themselves deserve thanks. All are subservient, all wish to be my friend, to obey and to think little. People are children.

At midday he passed through a village. Children danced about in the lane in front of the clay huts. They played with pumpkin-stones and mussels. They shouted and wrestled with each other, but ran away timidly when the strange Samana appeared. At the end of the village, the path went alongside a brook, and at the edge of the brook a young woman was kneeling and washing clothes. When Siddhartha greeted her, she raised her head and looked at him with a smile, so that he could see the whites of her eyes shining. He called across a benediction, as is customary among travellers, and asked how far the road still was to the large town. Thereupon she stood up and came towards him, her moist lips gleaming attractively in her young face.

She exchanged light remarks with him, asked him if he had yet eaten, and whether it was true that the Samanas slept alone in the forest at night and were not allowed to have any women with them. She then placed her left foot on his right and made a gesture, such as a woman makes when she invites a man to that kind of enjoyment of love which the holy books call 'ascending the tree'. Siddhartha felt his blood kindle, and as he recognised his dream again at that moment, he stooped a little towards the woman and kissed the brown tip of her breast. Looking up he saw her face smiling, full of desire and her half-closed eyes pleading with longing.

Siddhartha also felt a longing and the stir of sex in him; but as he had never yet touched a woman, he hesitated a moment, although his hands were ready to seize her. At that moment he heard his inward voice and the voice said: "No!" Then all the magic disappeared from the young woman's smiling face; he saw nothing but the ardent glance of a passionate young woman. Gently he stroked her cheek and quickly disappeared from the disappointed woman into the bamboo wood.

Before evening of that day he reached a large town and he was glad, because he had a desire to be with people. He had lived in the woods for a long time and the ferry-man's straw hut, in which he had slept the previous night, was the first roof he had had over him for a long time.

Outside the town, by a beautiful unfenced grove, the wanderer met a small train of men and women servants loaded with baskets. In the middle, in an ornamented sedan chair carried by four people, sat a woman, the mistress, on red cushions beneath a coloured awning. Siddhartha stood still at the entrance to the grove and watched the procession, the men servants, the maids and the bas-kets. He looked at the sedan chair and the lady in it. Beneath heaped-up black hair he saw a bright, very sweet, very clever face, a bright red mouth like a freshly cut fig, artful eyebrows painted in a high arch, dark eyes, clever and observant, and a clear slender neck above her green and gold gown. The woman's hands were firm and smooth, long and slender, with broad gold bangles on her wrists.

Siddhartha saw how beautiful she was and his heart rejoiced. He bowed low as the sedan chair passed close by him, and raising himself again, gazed at the bright fair face, and for a moment into the clever arched eyes, and inhaled the fragrance of a perfume which he did not recognise. For a moment the beautiful woman nodded and smiled, then disappeared into the grove, followed by her servants.

And so, thought Siddhartha, I enter this town under a lucky star. He felt the urge to enter the grove immediately, but he thought it over, for it had just occurred to him how the men servants and maids had looked at him at the entrance, so scornfully, so distrustfully, so dismissing in their glance. I am still a Samana, he thought, still an ascetic and a beggar. I cannot remain one; I cannot enter the grove like this. And he laughed.

He enquired from the first people that he met about the grove and the woman's name, and learned that it was the grove of Kamala, the well-known courtesan, and that besides the grove she owned a house in the town.

Then he entered the town. He had only one goal. Pursuing it, he surveyed the town, wandered about in the maze of streets, stood still in places, and rested on the stone steps to the river. Towards evening he made friends with a barber's assistant, whom he had seen working in the shade of an arch. He found him again at prayer in the temple of Vishnu, where he related to him stories about Vishnu and Lakshmi. During the night he slept among the boats on the river, and early in the morning, before the first customers arrived in the shop, he had his beard shaved off by the barber's assistant. He also had his hair combed and rubbed with fine oil. Then he went to bathe in the river.

When the beautiful Kamala was approaching her grove late in the afternoon in her sedan chair, Siddhartha was at the entrance. He bowed and received the courtesan's greeting. He beckoned the servant who was last in the procession, and asked him to announce to his mistress that a young Brahmin desired to speak to her. After a time the servant returned, asked Siddhartha to follow him, conducted him silently into a pavilion, where Kamala lay on a couch, and left him.

"Did you not stand outside yesterday and greet me?" asked Kamala.

"Yes indeed. I saw you yesterday and greeted you."

"But did you not have a beard and long hair yesterday, and dust in your hair?"

"You have observed well, you have seen everything. You have seen Siddhartha, the Brahmin's son, who left his home in order to become a Samana, and who was a Samana for three years. Now, however, I have left that path and have come to this town, and the first person I met before I reached the town was you. I have come here to tell you, O Kamala that you are the first woman to whom Siddhartha has spoken without lowered eyes. Never again will I lower my eyes when I meet a beautiful woman."

Kamala smiled and played with her fan made of peacocks' feathers, and asked: "Is that all that Siddhartha has come to tell me?"

"I have come to tell you this and to thank you because you are so beautiful. And if it does not displease you, Kamala, I would like to ask you to be my friend and teacher, for I do not know anything of the art of which you are mistress."

Thereupon Kamala laughed aloud.

"It has never been my experience that a Samana from the woods should come to me and desire to learn from me. Never has a Samana with long hair and an old torn loin-cloth cloth come to me. Many young men come to me, including Brahmins' sons, but they come to me in fine clothes, in fine shoes; there is scent in their hair and money in their purses. That is how these young men come to me, O Samana."

Siddhartha said: "I am already beginning to learn from you. I already learned something yesterday. Already I have got rid of my beard, I have combed and oiled my hair. There is not much more that is lacking, most excellent lady: fine clothes, fine shoes and money in my purse. Siddhartha has undertaken to achieve more difficult things than these trifles and has attained them. Why should I not attain what I decided to undertake yesterday?—to be your friend and to learn the pleasures of love from you. You will find me an apt pupil, Kamala. I have learned more difficult things than what you have to teach me. So Siddhartha is not good enough for you as he is, with oil in his hair, but without clothes, without shoes and without money!"

Kamala laughed and said: "No, he is not yet good enough. He must have clothes, fine clothes, and fine shoes, and plenty of money in his purse and presents for Kamala. Do you know now, Samana from the woods? Do you understand?"

"I understand very well," cried Siddhartha. "How could I fail to understand when it comes from such a mouth? Your mouth is like a freshly cut fig, Kamala. My lips are also red and fresh, and will fit yours well, you will see. But tell me, fair Kamala, are you not at all afraid of the Samana from the forest, who has come to learn about love?"

"Why should I be afraid of a Samana, a stupid Samana from the forest, who comes from the jackals and does not know anything about women?"

"O, the Samana is strong and afraid of nothing. He could force you, fair maiden, he could rob you, he could hurt you."

"No, Samana, I am not afraid. Has a Samana or a Brahmin ever feared that someone could come and strike him and rob him of his knowledge, of his piety, of his power for depth of thought? No, because they belong to himself and he can only give of them what he wishes, and if he wishes. That is exactly how it is with Kamala and with the pleasures of love. Fair and red are Kamala's lips, but try to kiss them against Kamala's will, and not one drop of sweetness will you obtain from them—although they know well how to give sweetness. You are an apt pupil, Siddhartha, so learn also this. One can beg, buy, be presented with and find love in the streets, but it can never be stolen. You have misunderstood. Yes, it would be a pity if a fine young man like you misunderstood."

Siddhartha bowed and smiled. "You are right, Kamala, it would be a pity. It would be a very great pity. No, no drops of sweetness must be lost from your lips, nor from mine. So Siddhartha will come again when he has what he is lacking in—clothes, shoes and money. But tell me, fair Kamala, can you not give me a little advice?"

"Advice? Why not? Who would not willingly give advice to a poor, ignorant Samana who comes from the jackals in the forest?"

"Dear Kamala, where can I go in order to obtain these three things as quickly as possible?"

"My friend, many people want to know that. You must do what you have learned and obtain money, clothes and shoes for it. A poor man cannot obtain money otherwise."

"I can think, I can wait, I can fast."

"Nothing else?"

"Nothing. O yes, I can compose poetry. Will you give me a kiss for a poem?"

"I will do so if your poem pleases me. What is it called?"

After thinking a moment, Siddhartha recited this verse:

"Into her grove went the fair Kamala,
At the entrance to the grove stood the brown Samana.
As he saw the lotus flower,
Deeply he bowed.

Smiling, acknowledged Kamala,
Better, thought the young Samana
To make sacrifices to the fair Kamala
Than to offer sacrifices to the gods."

Kamala clapped her hands loudly, so that the golden bangles tinkled. "Your poetry is very good, brown Samana, and truly there is nothing to lose if I give you a kiss for it."

She drew him to her with her eyes. He put his face against hers and placed his lips against hers. Kamala kissed him deeply, and to Siddhartha's great astonishment, he felt how much she taught him, how clever she was, how she mastered him, repulsed him, lured him, and how after this long kiss, a long series of other kisses, all different, awaited him. He stood still, breathing deeply. At that moment he was like a child astonished at the fullness of knowledge and learning which unfolded itself before his eyes.

"Your poetry is a very good," said Kamala, "if I were rich I would give you money for it. But it will be hard for you to earn as much money as you want with poetry. For you will need much money if you want to be Kamala's friend."

"How you can kiss, Kamala!" stammered Siddhartha.

"Yes, indeed, that is why I am not lacking in clothes, shoes, bangles and all sorts of pretty things. But what are you going to do? Cannot you do anything else besides think, fast and compose poetry?"

"I also know the sacrificial songs," said Siddhartha, "but I will not sing them any more. I also know incantations, but I will not pronounce them any more. I have read the scriptures..."

"Wait," interrupted Kamala, "you can read and write?"

"Certainly I can. Many people can do that."

"Not most people. I cannot. It is very good that you know how to read and write, very good. You might even need the incantations."

At that moment a servant entered and whispered something in his mistress's ear.

"I have a visitor," said Kamala. "Hurry and disappear, Siddhartha, nobody must see you here. I will see you again tomorrow."

However, she ordered the servant to give the holy Brahmin a white gown. Without quite knowing what was happening, Siddhartha was led away by the servant, conducted by a circuitous route to a garden house, presented with a gown, let into the thicket and expressly instructed to leave the grove unseen, as quickly as possible.

Contentedly, he did what he was told. Accustomed to the forest, he made his way silently out of the grove and over the hedge. Contentedly, he returned to the town, carrying his rolled-up gown under his arm. He stood at the door of an inn where travellers met, silently begged for food and silently accepted a piece of rice cake. Perhaps tomorrow, he thought, I will not need to beg for food.

He was suddenly overwhelmed with a feeling of pride. He was a Samana no longer; it was no longer fitting that he should beg. He gave the rice cake to a dog and remained without food.

The life that is lived here is simple, thought Siddhartha. It has no difficulties. Everything was difficult, irksome and finally hopeless when I was a Samana. Now everything is easy, as easy as the instruction in kissing, which Kamala gives. I require clothes and money, that is all. These are easy goals, which do not disturb one's sleep.

He had long since enquired about Kamala's town house and called there the next day.

"Things are going well," she called across to him. "Kamaswami expects you to call on him; he is the richest merchant in the town. If you please him, he will take you into his service. Be clever, brown Samana! I had your name mentioned to him through others. Be friendly towards him; he is very powerful, but do not be too modest. I do not want you to be his servant, but his equal; otherwise I shall not be pleased with you. Kamaswami is beginning to grow old and indolent. If you please him, he will place great confidence in you."

Siddhartha thanked her and laughed, and when she learned that he had not eaten that day, nor the previous day, she ordered bread and fruit to be brought to him and attended him.

"You have been lucky," she said to him on parting, "one door after the other is being opened to you. How does that come about? Have you a charm?"

Siddhartha said: "Yesterday I told you I knew how to think, to wait and to fast, but you did not consider these useful. But you will see that they are very useful, Kamala. You will see that the stupid Samanas in the forest learn and know many useful things. The day before yesterday I was still an unkempt beggar; yesterday I had already kissed Kamala and soon I will be a merchant and have money and all those things which you value."

"Quite," she agreed, "but how would you have fared without me? Where would you be now if Kamala had not helped you?"

"My dear Kamala," said Siddhartha, "when I came to you in your grove I made the first step. It was my intention to learn about love from the most beautiful woman. From the moment I made that resolution I also knew that I would execute it. I knew that you would help me; I knew it from your first glance at the entrance to the grove."

"And if I had not wanted?"

"But you did want. Listen, Kamala, when you throw a stone into the water, it finds the quickest way to the bottom of the water. It is the same when Siddhartha has an aim, a goal. Siddhartha does nothing; he waits, he thinks, he fasts, but he goes through the affairs of the world like the stone through the water, without doing any-thing, without bestirring himself; he is drawn and lets himself fall. He is drawn by his goal, for he does not allow anything to enter his mind that opposes his goal. That is what Siddhartha learned from the Samanas. It is what fools call magic and what they think is caused by demons. Nothing is caused by demons; there are no demons. Everyone can perform magic, everyone can reach his goal, if he can think, wait and fast."

Kamala listened to him. She loved his voice; she loved the look in his eyes.

"Perhaps it is as you say, my friend," she said softly, "and perhaps it is also because Siddhartha is a handsome man, because his glance pleases women, that he is lucky."

Siddhartha kissed her and said good-bye. "May it be so, my teacher. May my glance always please you; may good fortune always come to me from you!"

Amongst the People

Siddhartha went to see Kamaswami, the merchant, and was shown into a rich house. Servants conducted him across costly carpets to a room where he waited for the master of the house.

Kamaswami came in, a supple, lively man, with greying hair, with clever, prudent eyes and a sensual mouth. Master and visitor greeted each other in a friendly manner.

"I have been told," the merchant began, "that you are a Brahmin, a learned man, but that you seek service with a merchant. Are you then in need, Brahmin, that you seek service?"

"No," replied Siddhartha, "I am not in need and I have never been in need. I have come from the Samanas, with whom I lived for a long time."

"If you come from the Samanas, how is it that you are not in need? Are not all the Samanas completely without possessions?"

"I possess nothing," said Siddhartha, "if that is what you mean. I am certainly without possessions, but of my own free will, so I am not in need."

"But how will you live if you are without possessions?"

"I have never thought about it, sir. I have been without possessions for nearly three years and I have never thought about on what I should live."

"So you have lived on the possessions of others?"

"Apparently. The merchant also lives on the possessions of others."

"Well spoken, but he does not take from others for nothing, he gives his goods in exchange."

"That seems to be the way of things. Everyone takes and everyone gives. Life is like that."

"Ah, but if you are without possessions, how can you give?"

"Everyone gives what he has. The soldier gives strength, the merchant goods, the teacher instruction, the farmer rice, the fisherman fish."

"Very well; what can you give? What have you learned that you can give?"

"I can think, I can wait, I can fast."

"Is that all?"

"I think that is all."

"And of what use are they? For example, fasting, what good is that?"

"It is of great value, sir. If a man has nothing to eat, Fasting is the most intelligent thing he can do. If, for instance, Siddhartha had not learned how to fast, he would have had to seek some kind of work today, either with you, or elsewhere, for hunger would have driven him. But as it is, Siddhartha can wait calmly. He is not impatient, he is not in need, he can ward off hunger for a long time and laugh at it. Therefore, fasting is useful, sir."

"You are right, Samana. Wait a moment."

Kamaswami went out and returned with a roll, which he handed to his guest and enquired, "Can you read this?"

Siddhartha looked at the roll, on which a sales agreement was written, and began to read the contents.

"Excellent," said Kamaswami, "and will you write something for me on this sheet?"

He gave him a sheet and a pen and Siddhartha wrote something and returned the sheet.

Kamaswami read, "Writing is good, thinking is better. Cleverness is good, patience is better."

"You write very well," the merchant praised him. "We shall still have plenty to discuss, but to-day I invite you to be my guest and to live in my house."

Siddhartha thanked him and accepted. He now lived in the merchant's house. Clothes and shoes were brought to him and a servant pre-pared him a bath daily. Splendid meals were served twice a day, but Siddhartha only ate once a day, and neither ate meat nor drank wine. Kama-swami talked to him about his business, showed him goods and warehouses and accounts. Siddhartha learned many new things; he heard much and said little. And remembering Kamala's words, he was never servile to the merchant, but compelled him to treat him as an equal and even more than his equal. Kamaswami conducted his business with care and often with passion, but Siddhartha regarded it all as a game, the rules of which he endeavoured to learn well, but which did not stir his heart.

He had not been long in Kamaswami's house before he was already taking a part in his master's business. Daily, however, at the hour she invited him, he visited the beautiful Kamala, in handsome clothes, in fine shoes and soon he also brought her presents. He learned many things from her wise red lips. Her smooth, gentle hand taught him many things. He, who was still a boy as regards love, and inclined to plunge into the depths of it blindly and insatiably, was taught by her that one cannot have pleasure without giving it. And that every gesture, every caress, every touch, every glance, every single part of the body has its secret which can give pleasure to one who can understand.

She taught him that lovers should not separate from each other after making love without admiring each other, without being conquered as well as conquering, so that no feeling of satiation or desolation arises nor the horrid feeling of misusing or having been misused. He spent wonderful hours with the clever, beautiful courtesan and became her pupil, her lover, her friend. Here with Kamala lay the value and meaning of his present life, not in Kamaswami's business.

The merchant passed on to him the writing of im-portant letters and orders, and grew accustomed to conferring with him about all the important affairs. He soon saw that Siddhartha understood little about rice and wool, shipping and trade, but that he had a happy knack and surpassed the merchant in calmness and equanimity, and in the art of listening and making a good impression on strange people. "This Brahmin," he said to a friend, "is no real merchant and will never be one; he is never absorbed in the business. But he has the secret of those people to whom

success comes by itself, whether it is due to being
born under a lucky star or whether it is magic, or
whether he has learned it from the Samanas. He
always seems to be playing at business; it never
makes much impression on him, it never masters
him, he never fears failure, he is never worried
about a loss."

The friend advised the merchant, "Give him a
third of the profits of the business which he con-
ducts for you, but let him share the same propor-
tion of losses if any arise. He will thus become
more enthusiastic."

Kamaswami followed his advice, but
Siddhartha was little concerned about it. If he
made a profit, he accepted it calmly; if he suffered a loss, he laughed and said, "Oh well, this
transaction has gone badly."

He did, in fact, seem indifferent about business. Once he travelled to a village in order to
buy a large rice harvest. When he arrived there,
the rice was already sold to another merchant.
However, Siddhartha remained in that village for
several days, entertained the farmers, gave money

to the children, attended a wedding and returned from the journey completely satisfied. Kamaswami reproached him for not returning immediately, for wasting time and money. Siddhartha replied, "Do not scold, my dear friend. Nothing was ever achieved by scolding. If a loss has been sustained, I will bear the loss. I am very satisfied with this journey. I have become acquainted with many people, I have become friendly with a Brahmin, children have sat on my knee, and farmers have showed me their fields. Nobody took me for a merchant."

"That is all very fine," admitted Kamaswami reluc-tantly, "but you are in fact a merchant. Or were you only travelling for your pleasure?"

"Certainly I travelled for my pleasure," laughed Siddhartha. "Why not? I have become acquainted with people and new districts. I have enjoyed friendship and confidence. Now, if I had been Kamaswami, I should have departed im-mediately, feeling very annoyed when I saw I was unable to make a purchase, and time and money would indeed have been lost. But I spent a num-

ber of good days, learned much, had much pleasure and did not hurt either others or myself
through annoyance or hastiness. If I ever go there
again, perhaps to buy a later harvest, or for some
other purpose, friendly people will receive me
and I will be glad that I did not previously display hastiness and displeasure. Anyway, let it
rest, my friend, and do not hurt yourself by scolding. If the day comes when you think that
Siddhartha is doing you harm, just say one word
and Sid-dhartha will go on his way. Until then,
however, let us be good friends."

The merchant's attempts to convince
Siddhartha that he was eating his, Kamaswami's,
bread were also in vain. Siddhartha ate his own
bread; moreover, they all ate the bread of others,
everybody's bread. Siddhartha was never concerned about Kamaswami's troubles and
Kamaswami had many troubles. If a transaction
threatened to be unsuccessful, if a consignment
of goods was lost, if a debtor appeared unable to
pay, Kamaswami could never persuade his col-
league that it served any purpose to utter troubled

or angry words, to form wrinkles on the forehead and sleep badly. When Kamaswami once reminded him that he had learned everything from him, he replied, "Do not make such jokes. I have learned from you how much a basket of fish costs and how much interest one can claim for lending money. That is your knowledge. But I did not learn how to think from you, my dear Kamaswami. It would be better if you learned that from me."

His heart was not indeed in business. It was useful in order to bring him money for Kamala, and it brought him more than he really needed. Moreover, Siddhartha's sympathy and curiosity lay only with people whose work, troubles, pleasures and follies were more unknown and remote from him than the moon. Although he found it so easy to speak to everyone, to live with everyone and to learn from everyone, he was very conscious of the fact that there was something which separated him from them, and this was due to the fact that he had been a Samana. He saw people living in a childish or animal-like way, which he both loved and despised. He saw them toiling, saw them suffer and grow grey about things that to him did not seem worth the price, for money, small pleasures and trivial honours. He saw them scold and hurt each other; he saw them lament over pains, at which the Samana laughs, and suffer deprivations which a Samana does not feel.

He accepted all that people brought to him. The merchant who brought him linen for sale was welcome, the debtor who sought a loan was welcome; the beggar was welcome who stayed an hour telling him the story of his poverty, and who was yet not as poor as any Samana. He did not treat the rich foreign merchant differently from the servant who shaved him and the peddlers, from whom he bought bananas and let himself be robbed of small coins. If Kamaswami came to him and told him his troubles or made him reproaches about a transaction, he listened curiously and attentively. He was amazed at him, tried to understand him, conceded to him a little where it seemed necessary and turned away from him to the next one who wanted him.

Many people came to him, many to trade with
him, many to deceive him, many to listen to him,
many to elicit his sympathy and many to listen to
his advice. He gave advice, he sympathised, he
gave presents, he allowed himself to be cheated
a little, and he occupied his thoughts with all this
game and the passion with which all men play it,
as much as he had previously occupied his
thoughts with the gods and Brahman.

At times he heard within him a soft, gentle
voice, which reminded him quietly, complained
quietly, so that he could hardly hear it. Then he
suddenly saw clearly that he was leading a strange
life, that he was doing many things that were only
a game, that he was quite cheerful and sometimes
experienced pleasure, but that real life was flowing past him and did not touch him. Like a player
who plays with his ball, he played with his business, with the people around him, watched them,
derived amusement from them; but with his heart,
with his real nature, he was not there. His real self
wandered elsewhere, far away, wandered on and

on invisibly and had nothing to do with his life. He was sometimes afraid of these thoughts and wished that he could also share their childish daily affairs with intensity, truly to take part in them, to enjoy and live their lives instead of only being there as an onlooker.

He visited the beautiful Kamala regularly, learned the art of love in which, more than anything else, giving and taking become one. He talked to her, learned from her, gave her advice and received advice. She understood him better than Govinda had once done. She was more like him.

Once he said to her, "You are like me; you are dif-ferent from other people. You are Kamala and no one else, and within you there is a stillness and sanctuary to which you can retreat at any time and be yourself, just as I can. Few people have that capacity and yet everyone could have it.

"Not all people are clever," said Kamala.

"It has nothing to do with that, Kamala," said Siddhartha. "Kamaswami is just as clever as I am and yet he has no sanctuary. Others have it who are only children in understanding. Most people, Kamala, are like a falling leaf that drifts and turns in the air, flutters, and falls to the ground. But a few others are like stars, which travel one defined path; no wind reaches them, they have within them selves their guide and path. Among all the wise men, of whom I know many, there was one who was perfect in this respect. I can never forget him. He is Gautama, the Illustrious One, who preaches this gospel. Thousands of young men hear his teachings every day and follow his instructions every hour, but they are all falling leaves; they have not the wisdom and guide within themselves."

Kamala looked at him and smiled. "You are talking about him again," she said. "Again you have Samana thoughts."

Siddhartha was silent, and they played the game of love, one of the thirty or forty different games which Kamala knew. Her body was as supple as a jaguar and a hunter's bow; whoever learned about love from her, learned many pleasures, many secrets. She played with Siddhartha for a long time, repulsed him, overwhelmed him, conquered him, rejoiced at her mastery, until he was overcome and lay exhausted at her side.

The courtesan bent over him and looked long at his face, into his eyes that had grown tired.

"You are the best lover that I have ever had," she said thoughtfully. "You are stronger than others, more supple, more willing. You have learned my art well, Siddhartha. Some day, when I am older, I will have a child by you. And yet, my dear, you have remained a Samana. You do not really love me, you love nobody. Is that not true?"

"Maybe," said Siddhartha wearily. "I am like you. You cannot love either, otherwise how could you practice love as an art? Perhaps people like us cannot love. Ordinary people can, that is their secret."

Samsara

For a long time Siddhartha had lived the life of the world without belonging to it. His senses, which he had deadened during his ardent Samana years, were again awakened. He had tasted riches, passion and power, but for a long time he remained a Samana in his heart. Clever Kamala had recognised this. His life was always directed by the art of thinking, waiting and fasting. The people of the world, the ordinary people, were still alien to him, just as he was apart from them.

The years passed by. Enveloped by comfortable circumstances, Siddhartha hardly noticed their passing. He had become rich. He had long possessed a house of his own and his own servants, and a garden at the outskirts of the town, by the river. People liked him; they came to him if they wanted money or advice. However, with the exception of Kamala, he had no close friends.

That glorious, exalted awakening which he had once experienced in his youth, in the days after Gautama's preach-ing, after the parting from Govinda, had gone. That alert expectation, that pride of standing alone without teachers and doctrines, that eager readiness to hear the divine voice within his own heart, had gradually become a memory, had passed. The only fountainhead which had once been near, and which had once sung loudly within him, now murmured softly in the distance. However, many things which he had learned from the Samanas, from Gautama, from his father from the Brahmins, he still retained for a long time: a moderate life, pleasure in thinking, hours of meditation, secret knowledge of the Self, of the eternal Self, that was neither body nor consciousness. Many of these he had retained; others were submerged and covered with dust.

Just as the potter's wheel, once set in motion, still turns for a long time and then turns only very slowly and stops, so did the wheel of the ascetic, the wheel of thinking, the wheel of discrimination still revolve for a long time in Siddhartha's soul. It still revolved, but slowly and hesitatingly, and it had nearly come to a standstill. Slowly, like moisture entering a dying tree trunk, slowly filling and rotting it, so did the world and inertia creep into Siddhartha's soul; it slowly filled his soul, made it heavy, made it tired, sent it to sleep. But on the other hand his senses became more awakened; they learned a great deal, experienced a great deal.

Siddhartha had learned how to transact business affairs, to exercise power over people, to amuse himself with women; he had learned to wear fine clothes, to command servants, to bathe in sweet-smelling waters. He had learned to eat sweets and carefully prepared foods, also fish and meat and fowl, spices and dainties, and to drink wine, which made him lazy and forgetful. He had learned to play dice and chess, to watch dancers, to be carried in sedan chairs, to sleep on a soft bed. But he had always felt different from and superior to the others; he had always watched them a little scornfully, with a slightly mocking disdain, with that disdain which a Samana always feels towards the people of the world.

If Kamaswami was upset, if he felt that he had been insulted, or if he was troubled with his business affairs, Siddhartha had always regarded him mockingly. But slowly and imperceptibly, with the passing of the seasons, his mockery and feeling of superior-ity diminished. Gradually, along with his growing riches, Siddhartha himself acquired some of the characteristics of the ordinary people, some of their childishness and some of their anxiety. And yet he envied them; the more he became like them, the more he envied them. He envied them the one thing that he lacked and that they had: the sense of im-portance with which they lived their lives, the depth of their pleasures and sorrows, the anxious but sweet happiness of their continual power to love.

These people were always in love with themselves, with their children, with honour or money, with plans or hope. But these he did not learn from them, these childlike pleasures and follies; he only learned the unpleasant things from them, which he despised. It happened more frequently that after a merry evening, he lay late in bed the following morning and felt dull and tired. He would become annoyed and impatient when Kamaswami bored him with his worries. He would laugh too loudly when he lost at dice. His face was still more clever and intellectual than other people's, but he rarely laughed, and gradually his face assumed the expressions which are so often found among rich people—the expressions of discontent, of sickliness, of displeasure, of idleness, of loveless-ness. Slowly the soul sickness of the rich crept over him.

Like a veil, like a thin mist, weariness settled on Siddhartha, slowly, every day a little thicker, every month a little darker, every year a little heavier. As a new dress grows old with time, loses its bright colour, becomes stained and creased, the hems frayed, and here and there weak and threadbare places appear, so had Siddhartha's new life which he had begun after his parting from

Govinda become old. In the same way it had lost
its colour and sheen with the passing of the years:
creases and stains had accumulated, and hidden
in the depths, here and there already appearing,
waited disillu-sionment and nausea. Siddhartha
did not notice it. He only noticed that the bright
and clear inward voice, that had once awakened
in him and had always guided him in his finest
hours, had become silent.

The world had caught him; pleasure, covet-
ousness, idleness, and finally also that vice that he
had always despised and scorned as the most
foolish—acquisitiveness. Property, possessions
and riches had also finally trapped him. They were
no longer a game and a toy; they had become a
chain and a burden. Siddhartha wandered along
a strange, twisted path of this last and most base
declivity through the game of dice. Since the time
he had stopped being a Samana in his heart,
Siddhartha began to play dice for money and jewels with increasing fervour, a game in which he
had previously smilingly and indulgently taken part

as a custom of the ordinary people. He was a formidable player; few dared play with him, for his stakes were so high and reckless. He played the game as a result of a heartfelt need.

He derived a passionate pleasure through the gambling away and squandering of wretched money. In no other way could he show more clearly and mockingly his contempt for riches, the false deity of a businessmen. So he staked high and unsparingly, hating himself, mocking himself. He won thousands, he threw thousands away, lost money, lost jewels, lost a country house, won again and lost again. He loved that anxiety, that terrible and oppressive anxiety which he experienced during the game of dice, during the suspense of high stakes. He loved this feeling and continually sought to renew it, to increase it, to stimulate it, for in this feeling alone did he experience some kind of happiness, some kind of excitement, some heightened living in the midst of his satiated, tepid, insipid existence.

And after every great loss he devoted himself to the procurement of new riches, went eagerly after business and pressed his debtors for payment, for he wanted to play again, he wanted to squander again, he wanted to show his contempt for riches again. Siddhartha became impatient at losses, he lost his patience with slow-paying debtors, he was no longer kind-hearted to beggars, and he no longer had the desire to give gifts and loans to the poor. He, who staked ten thousand on the throw of the dice and laughed, became more hard and mean in business, and sometimes dreamt of money at night. And whenever he awakened from this hateful spell, whenever he saw his face reflected in the mirror on the wall of his bedroom, grown older and uglier, whenever shame and nausea over took him, he fled again. He fled to a new game of chance, fled in confusion to passion, to wine, and from there back again to the urge for acquiring and hoarding wealth. He wore himself out in this senseless cycle, became old and sick.

Then a dream once reminded him. He had been with Kamala in the evening, in her lovely pleasure garden. They sat under a tree talking.

Kamala was speaking seriously, and grief and weariness were concealed behind her words. She had asked him to tell her about Gautama, and could not hear enough about him, how clear his eyes were, how peaceful and beautiful his mouth, how gracious his smile, how peaceful his entire manner. For a long time he had talked to her about the Illustrious Buddha and Kamala had sighed and said, "One day, perhaps soon, I will also become a follower of this Buddha. I will give him my pleasure garden and take refuge in his teachings."

But then she enticed him, and in love play she clasped him to her with extreme fervour, fiercely and tearfully, as if she wanted once more to extract the last sweet drop from this fleeting pleasure. Never had it been so strangely clear to Siddhartha how closely related passion was to death. Then he lay beside her and Kamala's face was near to his, and under her eyes and near the corners of her mouth, he read clearly for the first time a sad sign—fine lines and wrinkles, a sign which gave a reminder of autumn and old age. Siddhartha himself, who was only in his forties, had noticed grey hairs here and there in his black hair. Weariness was written on Kamala's beautiful face, weariness from continuing along a long path which had no joyous goal, weariness and incipient old age, and concealed and not yet mentioned, perhaps a not yet conscious fear, fear of the autumn of life, fear of old age, fear of death. Sighing, he took leave of her, his heart full of misery and secret fear.

Then Siddhartha had spent the night at his house with dancers and wine, had pretended to be superior to his companions, which he no longer was. He had drunk much wine and late after midnight he went to bed, tired and yet agitated, nearly in tears and in despair. In vain did he try to sleep. His heart was so full of misery, he felt he could no longer endure it. He was full of nausea, which overpowered him like a distasteful wine, or music that was too sweet and superficial, or like the too sweet smile of the dancers or the too sweet perfume of their hair and breasts. But above all he was nauseated with himself, with his perfumed hair, with the smell of wine from his mouth, with

111

the soft, flabby appearance of his skin. Like one who has eaten and drunk too much and vomits pain-fully and then feels better, so did the restless man wish he could rid himself with one terrific heave of these pleasures, of these habits of this entirely senseless life. Only at daybreak and at the first signs of activity outside his town house, did he doze off and have a few moments of half-oblivion, a possibility of sleep. During that time he had a dream.

Kamala kept a small rare songbird in a small golden cage. It was about this bird that he dreamt. This bird, which usually sang in the morning, became mute, and as this surprised him, he went up to the cage and looked inside. The little bird was dead and lay stiff on the floor. He took it out, held it a moment in his hand and then threw it away on the road, and at the same moment he was horrified and his heart ached as if he had thrown away with this dead bird all that was good and of value in himself.

Awakening from this dream, he was overwhelmed by a feeling of great sadness. It seemed to him that he had spent his life in a worthless and senseless manner; he retained nothing vital, nothing in any way precious or worthwhile. He stood alone, like a shipwrecked man on the shore.

Sadly, Siddhartha went to a pleasure garden that belonged to him, closed the gates, sat under a mango tree, and felt horror and death in his heart. He sat and felt himself dying, withering, and finishing. Gradually, he collected his thoughts and mentally went through the whole of his life, from the earliest days which he could remember. When had he really been happy? When had he really experienced joy? Well, he had experienced this several times. He had tasted it in the days of his boyhood, when he had won praise from the Brahmins, when he far out stripped his contemporaries, when he excelled himself at the recitation of the holy verses, in argument with the learned men, when assisting at the sacrifices.

Then he had felt in his heart, "A path lies before you, which you are called to follow. The gods await you." And again as a youth, when his continually soaring goals had propelled him in and out of the crowd of similar seekers. And when he had striven hard to understand the Brahmins' teachings, when every freshly acquired knowledge only engendered a new thirst, then again, in the midst of his thirst, in the midst of his efforts, he had thought, "Onwards, onwards, this is your path." He had heard this voice when he had left his home and chosen the life of the Samanas, and again when he had left the Samanas and gone to the Perfect One, and also when he had left him for the unknown.

How long was it now since he had heard this voice, since he had soared to any heights? How flat and desolate his path had been! How many long years he had spent without any lofty goal, without any thirst, without any exaltation, content with small pleasures and yet never really satisfied. Without knowing it, he had endeavoured and longed all these years to be like all these other people, like these children, and yet his life had been much more wretched and poorer than theirs, for their aims were not his, nor their sorrows his. This whole world of the Kamaswami people had only been a game to him, a dance, a comedy, which one watches.

Only Kamala was dear to him, had been of value to him, but was she still? Did he still need her and did she still need him? Were they not playing a game without an end? Was it necessary to live for it? No. This game was called Samsara, a game for children, a game, which was perhaps enjoyable played once, twice, ten times, but was it worth playing continually?

Then Siddhartha knew that the game was finished; that he could play it no longer. A shudder passed through his body; he felt as if something had died.

He sat all that day under the mango tree, thinking of his father, thinking of Govinda, thinking of Gautama. Had he left all these in order to become a Kamaswami? He sat there until night fell. When he looked up and saw the stars, he thought, I am sitting here under my mango tree, in my pleasure garden. He smiled a little. Was it necessary, was it right, and was it not a foolish thing that he should possess a mango tree and a garden?

He had finished with that. That also died in him. He rose, said farewell to the mango tree and the pleasure garden. As he had not had any food that day he felt extremely hungry, and thought of his house in the town, of his room and bed, of the table with food. He smiled wearily, shook his head and said goodbye to these things.

The same night Siddhartha left his garden and the town and never returned. For a long time Kamaswami tried to find him, believing he had fallen into the hands of bandits. Kamala did not try to find him. She was not surprised when she learned that Siddhartha had disappeared. Had she not always expected it? Was he not a Samana, without a home, a pilgrim? She had felt it more than ever at their last meeting, and in the midst of her pain at her loss, she rejoiced that she had pressed him so close to her heart on that last occasion, had felt so completely possessed and mastered by him.

When she heard the first news of Siddhartha's dis-appearance, she went to the window where she kept a rare songbird in a golden cage. She opened the door of the cage, took the bird out and let it fly away. For a long time she looked after the disappearing bird. From that day she received no more visitors and kept her house closed. After a time, she found that she was with child as a result of her last meeting with Siddhartha.

By the River

Siddhartha wandered into the forest, already far from the town, and knew only one thing—that he could not go back, that the life he had lived for many years was past, tasted and drained to a degree of nausea. The songbird was dead; its death, which he had dreamt about, was the bird in his own heart. He was deeply entangled in Samsara; he had drawn nausea and death to himself from all sides, like a sponge that absorbs water until it is full. He was full of ennui, full of misery, full of death; there was nothing left in the world that could attract him, that could give him pleasure and solace.

He wished passionately for oblivion, to be at rest, to be dead. If only a flash of lightning would strike him! If only a tiger would come and eat him! If there were only some wine, some poison, that would give him oblivion, that would make him forget, that would make him sleep and never awaken! Was there any kind of filth with which he had not besmirched himself, any sin and folly which he had not committed, any stain upon his soul for which he alone had not been responsible? Was it then still possible to live? Was it possible to take in breath again and again, to breathe out, to feel hunger, to eat again, to sleep again, to lie with women again? Was this cycle not exhausted and finished for him?

Siddhartha reached the long river in the wood, the same river across which a ferryman had once taken him when he was still a young man and had come from Gautama's town. He stopped at this river and stood hesitatingly on the bank. Fatigue and hunger had weakened him. Why should he go any further; where, and for what purpose? There was no more purpose; there was nothing more than a deep, painful longing to shake off this whole confused dream, to spit out this stale wine, to make an end of this bitter, painful life.

There was a tree on the riverbank, a coconut tree. Siddhartha leaned against it, placed his arm around the trunk and looked down into the green water that flowed beneath him. He looked down and was completely filled with a desire to let himself go and be submerged in the water. A chilly emptiness in the water reflected the terrible emptiness in his soul. Yes, he was at the end. There was nothing more for him but to efface himself, to destroy the unsuccessful structure of his life, to throw it away, mocked at by the gods. That was the deed, which he longed to commit, to destroy the form that he hated! Might the fishes devour him, this dog of a Siddhartha, this madman, this corrupted and rotting body, this sluggish and misused soul! Might the fishes and crocodiles devour him, might the demons tear him to little pieces!

With a distorted countenance he stared into the water. He saw his face reflected, and spat at it; he took his arm away from the tree trunk and turned a little, so that he could fall headlong and finally go under. He bent, with closed eyes—towards death.

Then from a remote part of his soul, from the past of his tired life, he heard a sound. It was one word, one syllable, which without thinking he spoke indistinctly, the ancient beginning and ending of all Brahmin prayers, the holy Om, which had the meaning of "the Perfect One" or "Perfection." At that moment, when the sound of Om reached Siddhartha's ears, his slumbering soul suddenly awakened and he recognised the folly of his action.

Siddhartha was deeply horrified. So that was what he had come to; he was so lost, so confused, so devoid of all reason, that he had sought death. This wish, this childish wish had grown so strong within him; to find peace by destroying his body. All the torment of these recent times, all the disillusionment, all the despair, had not affected him so much as it did the moment the Om reached his consciousness and he recognised his wretchedness and his crime.

"Om," he pronounced inwardly, and he was conscious of Brahman, of the 'indestructibleness' of life; he remembered all that he had forgotten, all that was divine.

But it was only for a moment, a flash. Siddhartha sank down at the foot of the coconut tree, overcome by fatigue. Murmuring "Om," he laid his head on the tree roots and sank into a deep sleep.

His sleep was deep and dreamless; he had not slept like that for a long time. When he awakened after many hours, it seemed to him as if ten years had passed. He heard the soft rippling of the water; he did not know where he was nor what had brought him there. He looked up and was surprised to see the trees and the sky above him. He remembered where he was and how he came to be there. He felt a desire to remain there for a long time. The past now seemed to him to be covered by a veil, extremely remote, very unimportant.

He only knew that his previous life (at the first moment of his return to consciousness his previous life seemed to him like a remote incarnation, like an earlier birth of his present Self) was

finished. That it was so full of nausea and wretchedness that he had wanted to destroy it, but that
he had come to himself by a river, under a coconut tree, with the holy word Om on his lips. Then
he had fallen asleep, and on awakening he looked
at the world like a new man. Softly he said the
word Om to himself, over which he had fallen
asleep, and it seemed to him as if his whole sleep
had been a long deep pronouncing of Om, thinking of Om, an immersion and penetration into Om,
into the nameless, into the Divine.

What a wonderful sleep it had been! Never
had a sleep so refreshed him, so renewed him, so
rejuvenated him! Perhaps he had really died,
perhaps he had been drowned and was reborn
in another form. No, he recognised himself, he
recognised his hands and feet, the place where
he lay and the Self in his breast, Siddhartha, self-
willed, individualistic. But this Siddhartha was
somewhat changed, renewed. He had slept won-
derfully. He was remarkably awake, happy and
curious.

Siddhartha raised himself and saw a monk in a yellow gown, with shaved head, sitting opposite him in the attitude of a thinker. He looked at the man, who had neither hair on his head nor a beard, and he had not been looking at him for long when he recognised in this monk, Govinda the friend of his youth, Govinda who had taken refuge in the Illustrious Buddha. Govinda had also aged, but he still showed the old characteristics in his face; eagerness, loyalty, curiosity, and anxiety. But when Govinda, feeling his glance, raised his eyes and looked at him, Siddhartha saw that Govinda did not recognise him. Govinda was pleased to find him awake. Apparently he had sat there a long time waiting for him to awaken, although he did not know him.

"I was sleeping," said Siddhartha. "How did you come here?"

"You were sleeping," answered Govinda, "and it is not good to sleep in such places where there are often snakes and animals from the forest prowling about. I am one of the followers of the Illustrious Gautama, the Buddha of Sakyamuni, and I am on a pilgrimage with a number of our order. I saw you lying asleep in a dangerous place, so I tried to awaken you, and then as I saw you were sleeping very deeply, I remained behind my brothers and sat by you. Then it seems that I, who wanted to watch over you, fell asleep myself. Weariness overcame me and I kept my watch badly. But now you are awake, so I must go and overtake my brothers."

"I thank you, Samana, for guarding my sleep. The followers of the Illustrious One are very kind, but now you may go on your way."

"I am going. May you keep well."

"I thank you, Samana."

Govinda bowed and said, "Goodbye."

"Goodbye, Govinda," said Siddhartha.

The monk stood still.

"Excuse me, Sir, how do you know my name?"

Thereupon Siddhartha laughed.

"I know you, Govinda, from your father's house and from the Brahmins' school, and from the sacrifices, and from our sojourn with the Samanas and from that hour in the grove of Jetavana when you swore allegiance to the Illustrious One."

"You are Siddhartha," cried Govinda aloud. "Now I recognise you and do not understand why I did not recognise you immediately. Greetings, Siddhartha, it gives me great pleasure to see you again."

"I am also pleased to see you again. You have watched over me during my sleep. I thank you once again, although I needed no guard. Where are you going, my friend?"

"I am not going anywhere. We monks are always on the way, except during the rainy season. We always move from place to place, live according to the rule, preach the gospel, collect alms and then move on. It is always the same. But where are you going, Siddhartha?"

Siddhartha said, "It is the same with me as it is with you, my friend. I am not going anywhere. I am only on the way. I am making a pilgrimage."

Govinda said: "You say you are making a pilgrimage and I believe you. But forgive me,
Siddhartha, you do not look like a pilgrim. You
are wearing the clothes of a rich man, you are
wearing the shoes of a man of fashion, and your
perfumed hair is not the hair of a pilgrim, it is not
the hair of a Samana."

"You have observed well, my friend; you see
everything with your sharp eyes. But I did not tell
you that I am a Samana. I said I was making a
pilgrimage and that is true."

"You are making a pilgrimage," said Govinda,
"but few make a pilgrimage in such clothes, in
such shoes and with such hair. I, who have been
wandering for many years, have never seen such
a pilgrim."

"I believe you, Govinda. But today you have
met such a pilgrim in such shoes and dress. Remember, my dear Govinda, the world of appearances is transitory, the style of our clothes and hair
is extremely transitory. Our hair and our bodies
are themselves transitory. You have observed cor-
rectly. I am wearing the clothes of a rich man. I am

wearing them because I have been a rich man, and I am wearing my hair like men of the world and fashion because I have been one of them."

"And what are you now, Siddhartha?"

"I do not know; I know as little as you. I am on the way. I was a rich man, but I am no longer and what I will be tomorrow I do not know."

"Have you lost your riches?"

"I have lost them, or they have lost me, I am not sure. The wheel of appearances revolves quickly, Govinda. Where is Siddhartha the Brahmin, where is Siddhartha the Samana, where is Siddhartha the rich man? The transitory soon changes, Govinda. You know that."

For a long time Govinda looked doubtfully at the friend of his youth. Then he bowed to him, as one does to a man of rank, and went on his way.

Smiling, Siddhartha watched him go. He still loved him, this faithful anxious friend. And at that moment, in that splendid hour, after his wonderful sleep, permeated with Om, how could he help but love someone and some-thing? That was just the magic that had happened to him during his sleep and the Om in him. He loved everything, he was full of joyous love towards everything that he saw. And it seemed to him that was just why he was previously so ill, because he could love nothing and nobody.

With a smile Siddhartha watched the departing monk. His sleep had strengthened him but he suffered great hunger, for he had not eaten for two days, and the time was long past when he could ward off hunger. Troubled, yet also with laughter, he recalled that time. He remembered that at that time he had boasted of three things to Kamala, three noble and invincible arts: fasting, waiting and thinking. These were his possessions, his power and strength, his firm staff. He had learned these three arts and nothing else during the diligent, assiduous years of his youth. Now he had lost them, he possessed none of them any more, neither fasting, nor waiting, nor thinking. He had exchanged them for the most wretched things, for the transitory, for the pleasures of the senses, for high living and riches. He had gone along a strange path. And now, it seemed that he had indeed become an ordinary person.

Siddhartha reflected on his state. He found it difficult to think; he really had no desire to, but he forced himself.

Now, he thought, that all these transitory things have slipped away from me again. I stand once more beneath the sun, as I once stood as a small child. Nothing is mine, I know nothing, I possess nothing, I have learned nothing. How strange it is! Now, when I am no longer young, when my hair is fast growing grey, when strength begins to diminish, now I am beginning again like a child. He had to smile again. Yes, his destiny was strange! He was going backwards, and now he again stood empty, naked and ignorant in the world. But he did not grieve about it; no, he even felt a great desire to laugh, to laugh at himself, to laugh at this strange foolish world!

Things are going backwards with you, he said to himself and laughed, and as he said it, his glance lighted on the river, and he saw the river also flowing continually backwards, singing merrily. That pleased him immensely; he smiled cheerfully at the river. Was this not the river in which he had once wished to drown himself, hundreds of years ago, or had he dreamt it?

How strange his life had been, he thought. He had wandered along strange paths. As a boy I was occupied with the gods and sacrifices, as a youth with asceticism, with thinking and meditation. I was in search of Brahman and revered the eternal in Atman. As a young man I was attracted to expiation. I lived in the woods, suffered heat and cold. I learned to fast, I learned to conquer my body. I then discovered with wonder the teachings of the great Buddha. I felt knowledge and the unity of the world circulate in me like my own blood, but I also felt compelled to leave the Buddha and the great knowledge. I went and learned the pleasures of love from Kamala and business from Kamaswami. I hoarded money, I squandered money, I acquired a taste for rich food, I learned to stimulate my senses. I had to spend many years like that in order to lose my intelligence, to lose the power to think, to forget about the unity of things.

Is it not true, that slowly and through many deviations I changed from a man into a child? From a thinker into an ordinary person? And yet this path has been good and the bird in my breast has not died. But what a path it has been! I have had to experience so much stupidity, so many vices, so much error, so much nausea, disillusionment and sorrow, just in order to become a child again and begin anew. But it was right that it should be so; my eyes and heart acclaim it. I had to experience despair, I had to sink to the greatest mental depths, to thoughts of suicide, in order to experience grace, to hear Om again, to sleep deeply again and to awaken refreshed again. I had to become a fool again in order to find Atman in myself. I had to sin in order to live again. Whither will my path yet lead me? This path is stupid, it goes in spirals, perhaps in circles, but whichever way it goes, I will follow it.

He was aware of a great happiness mounting within him. Where does it come from, he asked himself? What is the reason for this feeling of happiness? Does it arise from my good long sleep, which has done me so much good? Or from the word Om which I pronounced? Or because I have run away, because my flight is accomplished, because I am at last free again and stand like a child beneath the sky? Ah, how good this flight has been, this liberation! In the place from which I escaped there was always an atmosphere of pomade, spice, excess and inertia. How I hated that world of riches, carousing and playing! How I hated myself for remaining so long in that horrible world! How I hated myself, thwarted, poisoned and tortured myself, made myself old and ugly. Never again, as I once fondly imagined, will I consider that Siddhartha is clever.

But one thing I have done well, which pleases me, which I must praise. I have now put an end to that self-detestation, to that foolish empty life. I commend you, Siddhartha, that after so many years of folly, you have again had a good idea, that you have accomplished something, that you have again heard the bird in your breast sing and followed it.

So he praised himself, was pleased with himself and listened curiously to his stomach, which rumbled from hunger. He felt he had thoroughly tasted and ejected a portion of sorrow, a portion of misery, during those past times, that he had consumed them up to a point of despair and death. But all was well.

He could have remained much longer with Kamaswami, made and squandered money, fed his body and neglected his soul. He could have dwelt for a long time yet in that soft, well-upholstered hell, if this had not happened, this moment of complete hopelessness and despair and the tense moment when he had bent over the flowing water, ready to commit suicide. This despair, this extreme nausea which he had experienced, had not overpowered him. The bird, the clear spring and voice within him was still alive, that was why he rejoiced, that was why he laughed, that was why his face was radiant under his grey hair.

It is a good thing to experience everything oneself, he thought. As a child I learned that the pleasures of the world and riches were not good. I have known it for a long time, but I have only just experienced it. Now I know it not only with my intellect, but with my eyes, my heart and my stomach. It is a good thing that I know this.

He thought long of the change in him, listened to the birds singing happily. If this bird within him had died, would he have perished? No, something else in him had died, something that he had long desired should perish. Was it not what he had once wished to destroy during his ardent years of asceticism? Was it not his Self, his small, fearful and proud Self, with which he had wrestled for so many years, but which had always conquered him again, which appeared each time again and again. That which robbed him of happiness and filled him with fear? Was it not this, which had finally died today in the wood by this delightful river? Was it not because of its death that he was now like a child, so full of trust and happiness, without fear?

Siddhartha now also realised why he had struggled in vain with this Self when he was a Brahmin and an ascetic. Too much knowledge had hindered him; too many holy verses, too many sacrificial rites, too much mortification of the flesh, too much doing and striving. He had been full of arrogance; he had always been the cleverest, the most eager, and always a step ahead of the others, always the learned and intellectual one, always the priest or the sage. His Self had crawled into this priesthood, into this arrogance, into this intellectuality. It sat there tightly and grew, while he thought he was destroying it by fasting and penitence.

Now he understood it and realised that the inward voice had been right, that no teacher could have brought him salvation. That was why he had had to go into the world, to lose himself in power, women and money; that was why he had had to be a merchant, a dice player, a drinker and a man of property, until the priest and Samana in him were dead. That was why he had had to undergo those horrible years, suffer nausea, learn the lesson of the madness of an empty, futile life till the end, till he reached bitter despair, so that Siddhartha the pleasure-monger and Siddhartha the man of property could die. He had died and a new Siddhartha had awakened from his sleep. He also would grow old and die. Siddhartha was transitory, all forms were transitory, but today he was young, he was a child, the new Siddhartha, and he was very happy.

These thoughts passed through his mind. Smiling, he listened to his stomach, listened thankfully to a humming bee. Happily he looked into the flowing river. Never had a river attracted him as much as this one. Never had he found the voice and appearance of flowing water so beautiful. It seemed to him as if the river had something special to tell him, something that he did not know, something that still awaited him. Siddhartha had wanted to drown himself in this river; the old, tired, despairing Siddhartha was today drowned in it. The new Siddhartha felt a deep love for this flowing water and decided that he would not leave it again so quickly.

The Ferryman

I will remain by this river, thought Siddhartha. It is the same river that I crossed on my way to the town. A friendly ferryman took me across. I will go to him. My path once led from his hut to a new life which is now old and dead. May my present path, my new life, start from there!

He looked lovingly into the flowing water, into the transparent green, into the crystal lines of its wonderful design. He saw bright pearls rise from the depths, bubbles swimming on the mirror, sky blue reflected in them. The river looked at him with a thousand eyes, green, white, crystal, sky blue. How he loved this river, how it enchanted him, how grateful he was to it! In his heart he heard the newly awakened voice speak, and it said to him, "Love this river, stay by it, learn from it." Yes, he wanted to learn from it, he wanted to listen to it. It seemed to him that whoever understood this river and its secrets would understand much more, many secrets, all secrets.

But today he saw only one of the river's secrets, one that gripped his soul. He saw that the water continually flowed and flowed and yet it was always there; it was always the same and yet every moment it was new. Who could understand, conceive this? He did not understand it; he was only aware of a dim suspicion, a faint memory and divine voices.

Siddhartha rose; the pangs of hunger were becoming unbearable. He wandered painfully along the riverbank, listening to the rippling of the water, listening to the gnawing hunger in his body.

When he reached the ferry, the boat was already there and the ferryman who had once taken the young Samana across stood in the boat. Siddhartha recognised him. He had also aged very much.

"Will you take me across?" he asked.

The ferrymen, astonished to see such a distinguished looking man alone and on foot, took him into the boat and set off.

"You have chosen a splendid life," said Siddhartha. "It must be fine to live near this river and sail on it every day."

The rower smiled, swaying gently.

"It is fine, Sir, as you say, but is not every life, every work fine?"

"Maybe, but I envy you yours."

"Oh, you would soon lose your taste for it. It is not for people in fine clothes."

Siddhartha laughed. "I have already been judged by my clothes today and regarded with suspicion. Will you accept these clothes from me, which I find a nuisance? For I must tell you that I have no money to pay you for taking me across the river."

"The gentleman is joking," laughed the ferryman.

"I am not joking, my friend. You once previously took me across this river without payment, so please do it today also and take my clothes instead."

"And will the gentleman continue without clothes?"

"I should prefer not to go further. I should prefer it if you would give me some old clothes and keep me here as your assistant, or rather your apprentice, for I must learn how to handle the boat."

The ferryman looked keenly at the stranger for a long time.

"I recognise you," he said finally. "You once slept in my hut. It is a long time ago, maybe more than twenty years ago. I took you across the river and we parted good friends. Were you not a Samana? I cannot remember your name."

"My name is Siddhartha and I was a Samana when you last saw me."

"You are welcome, Siddhartha. My name is Vasudeva. I hope you will be my guest today and also sleep in my hut; tell me where you have come from and why you are so tired of your fine clothes."

They had reached the middle of the river and Va-sudeva rowed more strongly because of the current. He rowed calmly, with strong arms, watching the end of the boat. Siddhartha sat and watched him and remembered how once, in those last Samana days, he had felt affection for this man. He gratefully accepted Vasudeva's invitation. When they reached the riverbank, he helped him to secure the boat. Then Vasudeva led him into the hut, offering him bread and water, which Siddhartha ate with enjoyment, as well as the mango fruit which Vasudeva offered him.

Later, when the sun was beginning to set, they sat on a tree trunk by the river and Siddhartha told him about his origin and his life and how he had seen him today after that hour of despair. The story lasted late into the night.

Vasudeva listened with great attention; he heard all about his origin and childhood, about his studies, his seeking, his pleasures and needs. It was one of the ferryman's greatest virtues that like few people, he knew how to listen. Without his saying a word, the speaker felt that Vasudeva took in every word, quietly, expectantly, that he missed nothing. He did not await anything with impatience and gave neither praise nor blame; he only listened. Siddhartha felt how wonderful it was to have such a listener who could be absorbed in another person's life, his strivings, and his sorrows.

However, towards the end of Siddhartha's story, when he told him about the tree by the river and his deep despair, about the holy Om, and how after his sleep he felt such a love for the river, the ferryman listened with doubled attention, completely absorbed, his eyes closed.

When Siddhartha had finished and there was a long pause, Vasudeva said, "It is as I thought; the river has spoken to you. It is friendly towards you, too; it speaks to you. That is good, very good. Stay with me, Siddhartha, my friend. I once had a wife; her bed was at the side of mine, but she died long ago. I have lived alone for a long time. Come and live with me; there is room and food for both of us."

"I thank you," said Siddhartha, "I thank you and accept. I also thank you, Vasudeva, for listening so well. There are few people who know how to listen and I have not met anybody who can do so like you. I will also learn from you in this respect."

"You will learn it," said Vasudeva, "but not from me. The river has taught me to listen; you will learn from it, too. The river knows everything; one can learn everything from it. You have already learned from the river that it is good to strive downwards, to sink, to seek the depths. The rich and distinguished Siddhartha will become a rower; Siddhartha the learned Brahmin will become a ferryman. You have also learned this from the river. You will learn the other thing, too."

After a long pause, Siddhartha said: "What other thing, Vasudeva?" Vasudeva rose. "It has grown late," he said, "let us go to bed. I cannot tell you what the other thing is, my friend. You will find out, perhaps you already know. I am not a learned man; I do not know how to talk or think.

I only know how to listen and be devout; otherwise I have learned nothing. If I could talk and teach I would perhaps be a teacher, but as it is I am only a ferryman and it is my task to take people across this river. I have taken thousands of people across and to all of them my river has been nothing but a hindrance on their journey.

"They have travelled for money and business, to weddings and on pilgrimages; the river has been in their way and the ferryman was there to take them quickly across the obstacle. However, amongst the thousands there have been a few, four or five, to whom the river was not an obstacle. They have heard its voice and listened to it, and the river has become holy to them, as it has to me. Let us now go to bed, Siddhartha."

Siddhartha stayed with the ferryman and learned how to look after the boat, and when there was nothing to do at the ferry, he worked in the rice field with Vasudeva, gathered wood, and picked fruit from the banana trees. He learned how to make oars, how to improve the boat and to make baskets. He was pleased with everything that he did and learned and the days and months passed quickly. But he learned more from the river than Vasudeva could teach him. He learned from it continually. Above all, he learned from it how to listen, to listen with a still heart, with a waiting, open soul, without passion, without desire, without judgement, without opinions.

He lived happily with Vasudeva and occasionally they exchanged words, few and long-considered words. Vasudeva was no friend of words. Siddhartha was rarely successful in moving him to speak.

He once asked him, "Have you also learned that secret from the river; that there is no such thing as time?"

A bright smile spread over Vasudeva's face.

"Yes, Siddhartha," he said. "Is this what you mean, that the river is everywhere, at the same time, at the source and at the mouth. It is at the waterfall, at the ferry, at the current, in the ocean and in the mountains, everywhere, and that the present only exists for it, not the shadow of the past, nor the shadow of the future?"

"That is it," said Siddhartha, "and when I learned that, I reviewed my life and it was also a river. And Siddhartha the boy, Siddhartha the mature man and Siddhartha the old man, were only separated by shadows, not through reality. Siddhartha's previous lives were also not in the past, and his death and his return to Brahman are not in the future. Nothing was, nothing will be, everything has reality and presence."

Siddhartha spoke with delight. This discovery had made him very happy. Was then not all sorrow in time, all self-torment and fear in time? Were not all difficulties and evil in the world conquered as soon as one conquered time, as soon as one dispelled time? He had spoken with delight, but Vasudeva just smiled radiantly at him and nodded his agreement. He stroked Siddhartha's shoulder and returned to his work.

And once again when the river swelled during the rainy season and roared loudly, Siddhartha said, "Is it not true, my friend, that the river has very many voices? Has it not the voice of a king, of a warrior, of a bull, of a night bird, of a pregnant woman and a sighing man, and a thousand other voices?"

"It is so," nodded Vasudeva, "the voices of all living creatures are in its voice."

"And do you know," continued Siddhartha, "what word it pronounces when one is successful in hearing all its ten thousand voices at the same time?"

Vasudeva laughed joyously; he bent towards Siddhartha and whispered the holy Om in his ear. And this was just what Siddhartha had heard.

As time went on, his smile began to resemble the ferryman's; it was almost equally radiant, almost equally full of happiness, equally lighting up through a thousand little wrinkles, equally childish, equally senile. Many travellers, when seeing both ferrymen together, took them for brothers. Often they sat together in the evening on the tree trunk by the river. They both listened silently to the water, which to them was not just water, but the voice of life, the voice of Being, of perpetual Becoming.

And it sometimes happened that, while listening to the river, they both thought the same thoughts, perhaps of a conversation of the previous day, or about one of the travellers whose fate and circumstances occupied their minds. They thought of death, or their childhood; and when the river told them something good at the same moment, they looked at each other, both thinking the same thought, both happy at the same answer to the same question.

Something emanated from the ferry and from both ferrymen that many of the travellers felt. It sometimes happened that a traveller, after looking at the face of one of the ferrymen, began to talk about his life and troubles, confessed sins, asked for comfort and advice. It sometimes happened that someone would ask permission to spend an evening with them in order to listen to the river. It also happened that curious people came along, who had been told that two wise men, magicians or holy men, lived at the ferry. The curious ones asked many questions but they received no replies, and they found neither magicians nor wise men. They only found two friendly old men, who appeared to be mute, rather odd and stupid. And the curious ones laughed and said how foolish and credible people were to spread such wild rumours.

The years passed and nobody counted them. Then one day, some monks came along, followers of Gautama, the Buddha, and asked to be taken across the river. The ferrymen learned from them that they were returning to their great teacher as quickly as possible, for the news had spread that the Illustrious One was seriously ill and would soon suffer his last mortal death and attain salvation. Not long afterwards another party of monks arrived and then another, and the monks as well as most of the other travellers talked of nothing but Gautama and his approaching death. And as people come from all sides to a military expedition or to the crowning of a king, so did they gather together like swarms of bees, drawn together by a magnet. They came to go to where the great Buddha was lying on his deathbed, where this great event was taking place and where the saviour of an age was passing into eternity.

Siddhartha thought a great deal at this time about the dying sage whose voice had stirred thousands, whose voice he had also once heard, whose holy countenance he had also once looked at with awe. He thought lovingly of him, remembered his path to salvation, and, smiling, remembered the words he had once uttered as a young man to the Illustrious One. It seemed to him that they had been arrogant and precocious words. For a long time he knew that he was not separated from Gautama, although he could not accept his teachings. No, a true seeker could not accept any teachings, not if he sincerely wished to find something. But he who had found, could give his approval to every path, every goal; nothing separated him from all the other thousands who lived in eternity, who breathed the Divine.

One day, when very many people were making a pilgrimage to the dying Buddha, Kamala, once the most beautiful of courtesans, was also on her way. She had long retired from her previous way of life, had presented her garden to Gautama's monks, taking refuge in his teachings, and belonged to the women and benefactresses attached to the pilgrims. On hearing of Gautama's approaching death, she had set off on foot, wearing simple clothes, together with her son.

They had reached the river on her way, but the boy soon became tired; he wanted to go home, he wanted to rest, he wanted to eat. He was often sulky and tearful. Kamala frequently had to rest with him. He was used to matching his will against hers. She had to feed him, comfort him, and scold him. He could not understand why his mother had to make this weary, miserable pilgrimage to an unknown place, to a strange man who was holy and was dying. Let him die; what did it matter to the boy?

The pilgrims were not far from Vasudeva's ferry, when little Siddhartha told his mother he wanted to rest. Kamala herself was tired, and while the boy ate a banana, she crouched down on the ground, half-closed her eyes and rested.

Suddenly, however, she uttered a cry of pain. The boy, startled, looked at her and saw her face white with horror. From under her clothes a small black snake, which had bitten Kamala, crawled away.

They both ran on quickly in order to reach some people. When they were near the ferry, Kamala collapsed and could not go any further. The boy cried out for help, meantime kissing and embracing his mother. She also joined in his loud cries, until the sounds reached Vasudeva, who was standing by the ferry. He came quickly, took the woman in his arms and carried her to the boat. The boy joined him and they soon arrived at the hut, where Siddhartha was standing and was just lighting the fire. He looked up and first saw the boy's face, which strangely reminded him of something. Then he saw Kamala, whom he recognised immediately, although she lay unconscious in the ferryman's arms. Then he knew that it was his own son whose face had so reminded him of something, and his heart beat quickly.

Kamala's wound was washed, but it was already black and her body had swelled. She was given a restorative and her consciousness returned. She was lying on Siddhartha's bed in his hut and Siddhartha, whom she had once loved so much, was bending over her. She thought she was dreaming, and smiling, she looked into her lover's face. Gradually, she realised her condition, remembered the bite and called anxiously for her son.

"Do not worry," said Siddhartha, "he is here."

Kamala looked into his eyes. She found it difficult to speak with the poison in her system. "You have grown old, my dear," she said, "you have become grey, but you are like the young Samana who once came to me in my garden, without clothes and with dusty feet. You are much more like him than when you left Kamaswami and me. Your eyes are like his, Siddhartha. Ah, I have also grown old, old, did you recognise me?"

Siddhartha smiled. "I recognised you immediately, Kamala, my dear."

Kamala indicated her son and said, "Did you recognise him, too? He is your son."

Her eyes wandered and closed. The boy began to cry. Siddhartha put him on his knee, let him weep and stroked his hair. Looking at the child's face, he remembered a Brahmin prayer, which he had once learned when he himself was a small child. Slowly and in a singing voice he began to recite it; the words came back to him out of the past and his childhood. The child became quiet as he recited, still sobbed a little and then fell asleep. Siddhartha put him on Vasudeva's bed. Vasudeva stood by the hearth cooking rice. Siddhartha looked at Vasudeva and smiled at him.

"She is dying," said Siddhartha softly.

Vasudeva nodded. The firelight from the hearth was reflected in his kind face.

Kamala again regained consciousness. There was pain in her face; Siddhartha read the pain on her mouth, in her pallid face. He read it quietly, attentively, waiting, sharing her pain. Kamala was aware of this; her glance sought his.

Looking at him, she said, "Now I see that your eyes have also changed. They have become quite different. How do I recognise that you are still Siddhartha? You are Siddhartha and yet you are not like him."

Siddhartha did not speak; silently he looked into her eyes.

"Have you attained it?" she asked. "Have you found peace?"

He smiled and placed his hand on hers.

"Yes," she said, "I see it. I also will find peace."

"You have found it," whispered Siddhartha.

Kamala looked at him steadily. It had been her intention to make a pilgrimage to Gautama, to see the face of the Illustrious One, to obtain some of his peace, and instead she had only found Siddhartha, and it was good, just as good as if she had seen the other. She wanted to tell him that, but her tongue no longer obeyed her will. Silently she looked at him and he saw the life fade from her eyes. When the last pain had filled and passed from her eyes, when the last shudder had passed through her body, his fingers closed her eyelids.

He sat there a long time looking at her dead face. For a long time he looked at her mouth, her old tired mouth and her shrunken lips, and remembered how once, in the spring of his life, he had compared her lips with a freshly cut fig.

For a long time he looked intently at the pale face, at the tired wrinkles and saw his own face like that, just as white, also dead. And at the same time he saw his face and hers, young, with red lips, with ardent eyes, and he was overwhelmed by a feeling of the present and contemporary existence. In this hour he felt more acutely the 'indestructibleness' of every life, the eternity of every moment.

When he rose, Vasudeva had prepared some rice for him but Siddhartha did not eat. In the stable, where the goat was, the two old men straightened some straw and Vasudeva lay down. But Siddhartha went outside and sat in front of the hut all night, listening to the river, sunk in the past, simultaneously affected and encompassed by all the periods of his life. From time to time, however, he rose, walked to the door of the hut and listened to hear if the boy were sleeping.

Early in the morning, before the sun was yet visible, Vasudeva came out of the stable and walked up to his friend.

"You have not slept," he said.

"No, Vasudeva, I sat here and listened to the river. It has told me a great deal, it has filled me with many great thoughts, with thoughts of unity."

"You have suffered, Siddhartha, yet I see that sadness has not entered your heart."

"No, my dear friend. Why should I be sad? I who was rich and happy have become still richer and happier. My son has been given to me."

"I also welcome your son. But now, Siddhartha, let us go to work, there is much to be done. Kamala died on the same bed where my wife died. We shall also build Kamala's funeral pyre on the same hill where I once built my wife's funeral pyre."

While the boy still slept, they built the funeral pyre.

The Son

Frightened and weeping, the boy had attended his mother's burial; frightened and gloomy, he had listened to Siddhartha greeting him as his son and making him welcome in Vasudeva's hut. For days on end he sat with a pale face on the hill of the dead, looked away, locked his heart, fought and strove against his fate.

Siddhartha treated him with consideration and left him alone, for he respected his grief. Siddhartha understood that his son did not know him, that he could not love him as a father. Slowly, he also saw and realised that the eleven-year-old child was a spoilt mother's boy and had been brought up in the habits of the rich, that he was accustomed to fine food and a soft bed, accustomed to commanding servants. Siddhartha understood that the spoilt and grieving boy could not suddenly be content in a strange and poor place. He did not press him; he did a great deal for him and always saved the best morsels for him. Slowly, by friendly patience, he hoped to win him over.

He had considered himself rich and happy when the boy had come to him. As time passed and the boy remained unfriendly, sulky, arrogant and defiant, did no work nor show any respect to the old people and robbed Vasudeva's fruit trees, Siddhartha began to realise that no happiness and peace had come to him with his son, only sorrow and trouble. But he loved him and preferred the sorrow and trouble of his love rather than happiness and pleasure without the boy.

Since young Siddhartha was in the hut, the old men had shared the work. Vasudeva had taken over all the work at the ferry and Siddhartha, in order to be with his son, the work in the hut and the fields.

For many months Siddhartha waited patiently in the hope that his son would come to understand him, that he would accept his love and that he would perhaps return it. For many months Vasudeva observed this, waited and was silent. One day, when young Siddhartha was distressing his father with his defiance and temper, and had broken both rice bowls, Vasudeva took his friend aside in the evening and talked to him.

"Forgive me," he said, "I am speaking to you as my friend. I can see that you are worried and unhappy. Your son, my dear friend, is troubling you, and also me. The young bird is accustomed to a different life, to a different nest. He did not run away from riches and the town with a feeling of nausea and disgust as you did; he has had to leave all these things against his will. I have asked the river, my friend, I have asked it many times, and the river laughed, it laughed at me and it laughed at you; it shook itself with laughter at our folly. Water will go to water, youth to youth. Your son will not be happy in this place. You ask the river and listen to what it says."

Troubled, Siddhartha looked at the kind face, in which there were many good-natured wrinkles.

"How can I part from him?" he said softly. "Give me time yet, my dear friend. I am fighting for him, I am trying to reach his heart. I will win him with love and patience. The river will also talk to him some day. He is also called."

Vasudeva's smile became warmer. "Oh yes," he said, "he is also called; he also belongs to the everlasting life. But do you and I know to what he is called, to which path, which deeds, which sorrows? His sorrows will not be slight. His heart is proud and hard. He will probably suffer much, make many mistakes, do much injustice and commit many sins. Tell me, my friend, are you educating your son? Is he obedient to you? Do you strike him or punish him?

"No, Vasudeva, I do not do any of these things."

"I knew it. You are not strict with him, you do not punish him, you do not command him, because you know that gentleness is stronger than severity, that water is stronger than rock, that love is stronger than force. Very good, I praise you. But is it not perhaps a mistake on your part not to be strict with him, not to punish him? Do you not chain him with your love? Do you not shame him daily with your goodness and patience and make it still more difficult for him? Do you not compel this arrogant, spoilt boy to live in a hut with two old banana eaters, to whom even rice is a dainty, whose thoughts cannot be the same as his, whose hearts are old and quiet and beat differently from his? Is he not constrained and punished by all this?

Siddhartha looked at the ground in perplexity. "What do you think I should do?" he asked softly.

Vasudeva said,"Take him into the town; take him to his mother's house. There will still be servants there; take him to them. And if they are no longer there, take him to a teacher, not just for the sake of education, but so that he can meet other boys and girls and be in the world to which he belongs. Have you never thought about it?"

"You can see into my heart," said Siddhartha sadly. "I have often thought about it. But how will he, who is so hard-hearted, go on in this world? Will he not consider himself superior, will he not lose himself in pleasure and power, will he not repeat all his father's mistakes, will he not perhaps be quite lost in Samsara?"

The ferryman smiled again. He touched Siddhartha's arm gently and said, "Ask the river about it, my friend! Listen to it, laugh about it! Do you then really think that you have committed your follies in order to spare your son them? Can you then protect your son from Samsara? How? Through instruction, through prayers, through exhortation? My dear friend, have you forgotten that instructive story about Siddhartha, the Brahmin's son, which you once told me here? Who protected Siddhartha the Samana from Samsara, from sin, greed and folly? Could his father's piety, his teacher's exhortations, his own knowledge, his own seeking, protect him? Which father, which teacher, could prevent him from living his own life, from soiling himself with life, from loading himself with sin, from swallowing the bitter drink himself, from finding his own path? Do you think, my dear friend, that anybody is spared this path? Perhaps your little son, because you would like to see him spared sorrow, pain and disillusionment? But if you were to die ten times for him, you would not alter his destiny in the slightest."

Never had Vasudeva talked so much. Siddhartha thanked him in a friendly fashion and went troubled to his hut, but could not sleep. Vasudeva had not told him anything that he had not already thought and known himself. But stronger than his knowledge was his love for the boy, his devotion, his fear of losing him. Had he ever lost his heart to anybody so completely; had he ever loved anybody so much, so blindly, so painfully, so hopelessly and yet so happily?

Siddhartha could not take his friend's advice; he could not give up his son. He allowed the boy to command him, to be disrespectful to him. He was silent and waited; he began daily the mute battle of friendliness and patience. Vasudeva was also silent and waited, friendly, understanding, forbearing. They were both masters of patience.

Once, when the boy's face reminded him of Kamala, Siddhartha suddenly remembered something she had once said to him a long time ago.

"You cannot love," she had said to him and he
had agreed with her. He had compared himself
with a star, and other people with falling leaves,
and yet he had felt some reproach in her words.
It was true that he had never fully lost himself in
another person to such an extent as to forget himself; he had never undergone the follies of love
for another person. He had never been able to
do this, and it had then seemed to him that this
was the biggest difference between him and the
ordinary people. But now, since his son was there,
he, Siddhartha, had become completely like one
of the people, through sorrow, through loving. He
was madly in love, a fool because of love. Now
he also experienced belatedly, for once in his life,
the strongest and strangest passion; he suffered
tremendously through it and yet was uplifted, in
some way renewed and richer.

He felt indeed that this love, this blind love
for his son, was a very human passion, that it was
Samsara, a troubled spring of deep water. At the
same time he felt that it was not worthless, that it
was necessary, that it came from his own nature.

This emotion, this pain, these follies also had to be experienced.

In the meantime, his son let him commit his follies, let him strive, let him be humbled by his moods. There was nothing about this father that attracted him and nothing that he feared. This father was a good man, a kind gentle man, perhaps a pious man, perhaps a holy man, but all these were not qualities which could win the boy. This father who kept him in this wretched hut bored him, and when he answered his rudeness with a smile, every insult with friendliness, every naughtiness with kindness, that was the most hateful cunning of the old fox. The boy would have much preferred him to threaten him, to illtreat him.

A day came when young Siddhartha said what was in his mind and openly turned against his father. The latter had told him to gather some twigs. But the boy did not leave the hut; he stood there, defiant and angry, stamped on the ground, clenched his fists and forcibly declared his hatred and contempt in his father's face.

"Bring your own twigs," he shouted, foaming. "I am not your servant. I know that you do not beat me; you dare not! I know, however, that you continually punish me and make me feel small with your piety and indulgence. You want me to become like you, so pious, so gentle, so wise, but just to spite you, I would rather become a thief and a murderer and go to hell, than be like you. I hate you; you are not my father even if you have been my mother's lover a dozen times!"

Full of rage and misery, he found an outlet in a stream of wild and angry words at his father. Then the boy ran away and only returned late in the evening. The following morning he had disappeared. A small two-coloured basket made of bast, in which the ferrymen kept the copper and silver coins which they received as their payment, had also disappeared. The boat, too, had gone. Siddhartha saw it on the other side of the bank. The boy had run away.

"I must follow him," said Siddhartha, who had been in great distress since the boy's hard words of the previous day. "A child cannot go through the forest alone; he will come to some harm. We must make a raft, Vasudeva, in order to cross the river."

"We will make a raft," said Vasudeva, "in order to fetch our boat which the boy took away. But let him go, my friend, he is not a child any more, he knows how to look after himself. He is seeking the way to the town and he is right. Do not forget that. He is doing what you yourself have neglected to do. He is looking after himself; he is going his own way. Oh, Siddhartha, I can see you are suffering, suffering pain over which one should laugh, over which you will soon laugh yourself."

Siddhartha did not reply. He already held the hatchet in his hands and began to build a raft from bamboo and Vasudeva helped him to bind the cane together with grass rope. Then they sailed across, were driven far out, but directed the raft upstream to the other bank.

"Why have you brought the hatchet with you?" asked Siddhartha.

Vasudeva said: "It is possible that the oar of our boat is lost."

But Siddhartha knew what his friend was thinking, probably that the boy would have thrown the oar away or broken it out of revenge and to prevent their following him. And indeed, there was no longer an oar in the boat. Vasudeva indicated the bottom of the boat and smiled at his friend as if to say: Do you not see what your son wishes to say? Do you not see that he does not wish to be followed? But he did not say it in words and started to make a new oar. Siddhartha took leave of him to look for the boy. Vasudeva did not hinder him.

Siddhartha had been in the forest a long time when the thought occurred to him that his search was useless. Either, he thought, the boy had long ago left the wood and reached the town, or if he were still on the way, he would hide from the pursuer. And when he reflected further, he found that he was not troubled about his son, that inwardly he knew he had neither come to any harm nor was threatened with danger in the forest. Nevertheless, he went on steadily, no longer to save him, but with a desire perhaps to see him again, and he walked up to the outskirts of the town.

When he reached the wide road near the town, he stood still at the entrance to the beautiful pleasure garden that had once belonged to Kamala, where he had once seen her in a sedan chair for the first time. The past rose before his eyes. Once again he saw himself standing there, a young, bearded, naked Samana, his hair full of dust. Siddhartha stood there a long time and looked through the open gate into the garden. He saw monks walking about under the beautiful trees.

He stood there for a long time, thinking, seeing pictures, seeing the story of his life. He stood there a long time looking at the monks, saw in their place the young Siddhartha and Kamala walking beneath the tall trees. Clearly he saw himself attended by Kamala and receiving her first kiss. He saw how he had arrogantly and contemptuously looked back on his Samana days, how he had proudly and eagerly begun his worldly life. He saw Kamaswami, the servants, the banquets, the dice players, the musicians. He saw

Kamala's songbird in its cage; he lived it all over again, breathed Samsara, was again old and tired, again felt nausea and the desire to die, again heard the holy Om.

After he had stood for a long time at the gate to the garden, Siddhartha realised that the desire that had driven him to this place was foolish, that he could not help his son, that he should not force himself on him. He felt a deep love for the runaway boy, like a wound, and yet felt at the same time that this wound was not intended to fester in him, but that it should heal.

Because the wound did not heal during that hour, he was sad. In place of the goal that had brought him here after his son, there was only emptiness. Sadly, he sat down. He felt something die in his heart; he saw no more happiness, no goal. He sat there depressed and waited. He had learned this from the river; to wait, to have patience, to listen. He sat and listened on the dusty road, listened to his heart, which beat wearily and sadly, and waited for a voice. He crouched there and listened for many hours; he saw no more visions, he just sank into emptiness and let himself sink without seeing a way out. And when he felt the wound smarting, he whispered the word Om, filled himself with Om. The monks in the garden saw him and, as he crouched there for many hours and the dust collected on his grey hair, one of the monks came towards him and placed two bananas in front of him. The old man did not see him.

A hand touching his shoulder awakened him from his trance. He recognised this gentle, timid touch and recovered. He rose and greeted Vasudeva, who had followed him. When he saw Vasudeva's kind face, looked at his little laughter wrinkles, into his bright eyes, he smiled also. He now saw the bananas lying near him. He picked them up, gave one to the ferryman and ate the other. Then he went silently with Vasudeva through the wood again, back to the ferry. Neither spoke of what had happened; neither mentioned the boy's name, neither spoke of his flight, nor of the wound. Siddhartha went to his bed in the hut and, when Vasudeva went to him after a time to offer him some coconut milk, he found him asleep.

Om

The wound smarted for a long time. Siddhartha took many travellers across the river who had a son or a daughter with them, and he could not see any of them without envying them, without thinking, "So many people possess this very great happiness, why not I? Even wicked people, thieves and robbers have children, love them and are loved by them, except me." So childishly and illogically did he now reason; so much had he become like the ordinary people.

He now regarded people in a different light than he had previously; not very clever, not very proud and there-fore all the more warm, curious and sympathetic.

When he now took the usual kind of travellers across, businessmen, soldiers and women, they no longer seemed alien to him as they once had. He did not understand or share their thoughts and views, but he shared with them life's urges and desires. Although he had reached a high stage of self-discipline and bore his last wound well, he now felt as if these ordinary people were his brothers. Their vanities, desires and trivialities no longer seemed absurd to him; they had become understandable, lovable and even worthy of respect. There was the blind love of a mother for her child, the blind foolish pride of a fond father for his only son, the blind eager strivings of a young vain woman for ornament and the admiration of men. All these little simple, foolish, but tremendously strong, vital, passionate urges and desires no longer seemed trivial to Siddhartha. For their sake he saw people live and do great things, travel, conduct wars, suffer and endure immensely, and he loved them for it. He saw life, vitality, the indestructible and Brahman in all their desires and needs. These people were worthy of love and admiration in their blind loyalty, in their blind strength and tenacity. With the exception of one small thing, one tiny little thing, they lacked nothing that the sage and thinker had, and that was the consciousness of the unity of all life. And many a time Siddhartha even doubted whether this knowledge, this thought, was of such great value, whether it was not also perhaps the childish self-flattery of thinkers, who were perhaps only thinking children. The men of the world were equal to the thinkers in every other respect and were often superior to them, just as animals in their tenacious undevi-ating actions in cases of necessity may often seem superior to human beings.

Within Siddhartha there slowly grew and ripened the knowledge of what wisdom really was and the goal of his long seeking. It was nothing but a preparation of the soul, a capacity, a secret art of thinking, feeling and breathing thoughts of unity at every moment of life. This thought matured in him slowly, and it was reflected in Vasudeva's old child-like face; harmony, knowledge of the eternal perfection of the world, and unity.

But the wound still smarted. Siddhartha thought yearningly and bitterly about his son, nursed his love and feeling of tenderness for him, let the pain gnaw at him, underwent all the follies of love. The flame did not extinguish itself.

One day, when the wound was smarting terribly, Siddhartha rowed across the river, consumed by longing, and got out of the boat with the purpose of going to the town to seek his son. The river flowed softly and gently; it was in the dry season but its voice rang out strangely. It was laughing; it was distinctly laughing! The river was laughing clearly and merrily at the old ferryman. Siddhartha stood still; he bent over the water in order to hear better. He saw his face reflected in the quietly moving water, and there was something in this reflection that reminded him of something he had forgotten and, when he reflected on it, he remembered.

His face resembled that of another person, whom he had once known and loved and even feared. It resembled the face of his father, the Brahmin. He remembered how once, as a youth, he had compelled his father to let him go and join the ascetics, how he had taken leave of him, how he had gone and never returned. Had not his father also suffered the same pain that he was now suffering for his son? Had not his father died long ago, alone, without having seen his son again? Did he not expect the same fate? Was it not a comedy, a strange and stupid thing, this repetition, this course of events in a fateful circle?

The river laughed. Yes, that was how it was. Everything that was not suffered to the end and finally concluded, recurred, and the same sorrows were undergone. Siddhartha climbed into the boat again and rowed back to the hut, thinking of his father, thinking of his son, laughed at by the river, in conflict with himself, verging on despair, and no less inclined to laugh aloud at himself and the whole world. The wound still smarted; he still rebelled against his fate. There was still no serenity and conquest of his suffering. Yet he was hopeful and, when he returned to the hut, he was filled with an unconquerable desire to confess to Vasudeva, to disclose every-thing, to tell everything to the man who knew the art of listening.

Vasudeva sat in the hut weaving a basket. He no longer worked the ferryboat; his eyes were becoming weak, also his arms and hands, but unchanged and radiant were the happiness and the serene well-being in his face.

Siddhartha sat down beside the old man and slowly began to speak. He told him now what he had never mentioned before, how he had gone to the town that time, of his smarting wound, of his envy at the sight of happy fathers, of his knowledge of the folly of such feelings, of his hopeless struggle with himself. He mentioned everything, he could tell him everything, even the most painful things; he could disclose everything. He displayed his wound, told him of his flight that day, how he had rowed across the river with the object of wandering into the town, and how the river had laughed.

As he went on speaking and Vasudeva lis-tened to him with a serene face, Siddhartha was more keenly aware than ever of Vasudeva's attentiveness. He felt his troubles, his anxieties and his secret hopes flow across to him and then return again. Disclosing his wound to this listener was the same as bathing it in the river, until it became cool and one with the river. As he went on talking and confessing, Siddhartha felt more and more that this was no longer Vasudeva, no longer a man who was listening to him. He felt that this motionless listener was absorbing his confession as a tree absorbs the rain, that this motionless man was the river itself, that he was God Himself, that he was eternity itself.

As Siddhartha stopped thinking about himself and his wound, this recognition of the change in Vasudeva possessed him. The more he realised it, the less strange did he find it; the more did he realise that everything was natural and in order, that Vasudeva had long ago, almost always been like that, only he did not quite recognise it. Indeed, he himself was hardly different from him. He felt that he now regarded Vasudeva as the people regarded the gods and that this could not last. Inwardly, he began to take leave of Vasudeva. In the meantime he went on talking.

When he had finished talking, Vasudeva directed his somewhat weakened glance at him. He did not speak, but his face silently radiated love and serenity, understanding and knowledge. He took Siddhartha's hand, led him to the seat on the riverbank, sat down beside him and smiled at the river.

"You have heard it laugh," he said, "but you have not heard everything. Let us listen; you will hear more."

They listened. The manyvoiced song of the river echoed softly. Siddhartha looked into the river and saw many pictures in the flowing water. He saw his father, lonely, mourning for his son; he saw himself, lonely also, with the bonds of longing for his faraway son. He saw his son, also lonely, the boy eagerly advancing along the burning path of life's desires. Each one was concentrating on his goal, each one obsessed by his goal, each one suffering.

The river's voice was sorrowful. It sang with yearning and sadness, flowing towards its goal.

"Do you hear?" asked Vasudeva's mute glance. Siddhartha nodded.

"Listen better!" whispered Vasudeva.

Siddhartha tried to listen better. The picture of his father, his own picture, and the picture of his son all flowed into each other. Kamala's picture also appeared and flowed on, and the picture of Govinda and others emerged and passed on. They all became part of the river. It was the goal of all of them, yearning, desiring, suffering; and the river's voice was full of longing, full of smarting woe, full of insatiable desire. The river flowed on towards its goal. Siddhartha saw the river hasten, made up of himself and his relatives and all the people he had ever seen. All the waves and water hastened, suffering, towards goals, many goals, to the waterfall, to the sea, to the current, to the ocean and all goals were reached and each one was succeeded by another. The water changed to vapour and rose, became rain and came down again, became springs, brooks and rivers, changed anew, flowed anew. But the yearning voice had altered. It still echoed sorrowfully, searchingly, but other voices accompanied it, voices of pleasure and sorrow, good and evil voices, laughing and lamenting voices, hundreds of voices, thousands of voices.

Siddhartha listened. He was now listening intently, completely absorbed, quite empty, taking in everything. He felt that he had now completely learned the art of listening. He had often heard all this before, all these numerous voices in the river, but today they sounded different. He could no longer distinguish the different voices, the merry voice from the weeping voice, the childish voice from the manly voice. They all belonged to each other; the lament of those who yearn, the laughter of the wise, the cry of indignation and the groan of the dying. They were all interwoven and interlocked, entwined in a thousand ways. And all the voices, all the goals, all the yearnings, all the sorrows, all the pleasures, all the good and evil, all of them together was the world. All of them together were the stream of events, the music of life.

When Siddhartha listened attentively to this river, to this song of a thousand voices, when he did not listen to the sorrow or laughter, when he did not bind his soul to any one particular voice and absorb it in his Self, but heard them all, the whole, the unity; then the great song of a thousand voices consisted of one word: Om—perfection.

"Do you hear?" asked Vasudeva's glance once again.

Vasudeva's smile was radiant; it hovered brightly in all the wrinkles of his old face, as the Om hovered over all the voices of the river. His smile was radiant as he looked at his friend, and now the same smile appeared on Siddhartha's face. His wound was healing, his pain was dispersing; his Self had merged into unity.

From that hour Siddhartha ceased to fight against his destiny. There shone in his face the serenity of knowledge, of one who is no longer confronted with conflict of desires. Of one who has found salvation, who is in harmony with the stream of events, with the stream of life, full of sympathy and compassion, surrendering himself to the stream, belonging to the unity of all things.

As Vasudeva rose from the seat on the river bank, when he looked into Siddhartha's eyes and saw the serenity of knowledge shining in them, he touched his shoulder gently in his kind protective way and said, "I have waited for this hour, my friend. Now that it has arrived, let me go. I have been Vasudeva, the ferryman, for a long time. Now it is over. Farewell hut, farewell river, farewell Siddhartha."

Siddhartha bowed low before the departing man. "I knew it," he said softly. "Are you going into the woods?"

"Yes, I am going into the woods; I am going into the unity of all things," said Vasudeva, radiant. And so he went away. Siddhartha watched him. With great joy and gravity he watched him, saw his steps full of peace, his face glowing, his form full of light.

Govinda

Govinda once spent a rest period with some other monks in the pleasure grove which Kamala, the courtesan, had once presented to the followers of Gautama. He heard talk of an old ferryman who lived by the river, a day's journey away, and whom many considered to be a sage. When Govinda moved on, he chose the path to the ferry, eager to see this ferryman. Although he had lived his life according to the rule and was also regarded with respect by the younger monks for his age and modesty, there was still restlessness in his heart and his seeking was unsatisfied.

He arrived at the river and asked the old man to take him across. When they climbed out of the boat on the other side, he said to the old man, "You show much kindness to the monks and pilgrims; you have taken many of us across. Are you not also a seeker of the right path?"

There was a smile in Siddhartha's old eyes as he said, "Do you call yourself a seeker, O venerable one, you who are already advanced in years and wear the robe of Gautama's monks?"

"I am indeed old," said Govinda, "but I have never ceased seeking. I will never cease seeking. That seems to be my destiny. It seems to me that you also have sought. Will you talk to me a little about it, my friend?

Siddhartha said, "What could I say to you that would be of value, except that perhaps you seek too much, that as a result of your seeking you cannot find?"

"How is that?" asked Govinda.

"When someone is seeking," said Siddhartha, "it hap-pens quite easily that he only sees the thing that he is seeking. He is unable to find anything, unable to absorb anything, because he is only thinking of the thing he is seeking, because he has a goal, because he is obsessed with his goal. Seeking means to have a goal, but finding means to be free, to be receptive, to have no goal. You, O worthy one, are perhaps indeed a seeker, for in striving towards your goal, you do not see many things that are under your nose."

"I do not yet quite understand," said Govinda. "How do you mean?"

Siddhartha said, "Once, O worthy one, many years ago, you came to this river and found a man sleeping there. You sat beside him to guard him while he slept, but you did not recognise the sleeping man, Govinda."

Astonished and like one bewitched the monk gazed at the ferryman. "Are you Siddhartha?" he asked in a timid voice. "I did not recognise you this time, either. I am very pleased to see you again, Siddhartha, very pleased. You have changed very much, my friend. And have you become a ferryman now?"

Siddhartha laughed warmly. "Yes, I have become a ferryman. Many people have to change a great deal and wear all sorts of clothes. I am one of those, my friend. You are very welcome, Govinda, and I invite you to stay the night in my hut."

Govinda stayed the night in the hut and slept in the bed that had once been Vasudeva's. He asked the friend of his youth many questions and Siddhartha had a great deal to tell him about his life.

When it was time for Govinda to depart the following morning, he said with some hesitation, "Before I go o n my way, Siddhartha, I should like to ask you one more question. Have you a doctrine, belief or knowledge which you uphold, which helps you to live and do right?"

Siddhartha said, "You know, my friend, that even as a young man, when we lived with the ascetics in the forest, I came to distrust doctrines and teachers and to turn my back on them. I am still of the same turn of mind, although I have, since that time, had many teachers. A beautiful cour-tesan was my teacher for a long time, and a rich merchant and a dice player. On one occasion, one of the Buddha's wandering monks was my teacher. He halted in his pil-grimage to sit beside me when I fell asleep in the forest. I also learned something from him and I am grateful to him, very grateful. But most of all, I have learned from this river and from my predecessor, Vasudeva. He was a simple man; he was not a thinker, but he realised the essential as well as Gautama. He was a holy man, a saint."

Govinda said, "It seems to me, Siddhartha that you still like to jest a little. I believe you and know that you have not followed any teacher, but have you not yourself, if not a doctrine, certain thoughts? Have you not discov-ered certain knowledge yourself that has helped you to live? It would give me great pleasure if you would tell me something about this."

Siddhartha said, "Yes, I have had thoughts and knowledge here and there. Sometimes, for an hour or for a day, I have become aware of knowledge, just as one feels life in one's heart. I have had many thoughts, but it would be difficult for me to tell you about them. But this is one thought that has impressed me, Govinda. Wisdom is not communicable. The wisdom that a wise man tries to communicate always sounds foolish.

"Are you jesting?" asked Govinda.

"No, I am telling you what I have discovered. Knowledge can be communicated, but not wisdom. One can find it, live it, be fortified by it, do wonders through it, but one cannot communicate and teach it. I suspected this when I was still a youth and it was this that drove me away from teachers. There is one thought I have had, Govinda, that you will again think is a jest or folly; that is, in every truth the opposite is equally true. For example, a truth can only be expressed and enveloped in words if it is one-sided. Everything that is thought and expressed in words is one-sided, only half the truth; it all lacks totality, completeness, unity. When the illustrious Buddha taught about the world, he had to divide it into Samsara and Nirvana, into illusion and truth, into suffering and salvation. One cannot do otherwise; there is no other method for those who teach. But the world itself, being in and around us, is never one-sided.

Never is a man or a deed wholly samsara or wholly nirvana; never is a man wholly a saint or a sinner. This only seems so because we suffer the illusion that time is something real. Time is not real, Govinda. I have realised this repeatedly. And if time is not real, then the dividing line that seems to lie between this world and eternity, between suffering and bliss, between good and evil, is also an illusion."

"How is that?" asked Govinda, puzzled.

"Listen, my friend! I am a sinner and you are a sinner, but someday the sinner will be Brahman again, will someday attain nirvana, and will someday become a Buddha. Now this 'someday' is illusion; it is only a comparison. The sinner is not on the way to a Buddha-like state; he is not evolving, although our thinking cannot conceive things otherwise. No, the potential Buddha already exists in the sinner; his future is already there. The potential hidden Buddha must be recognised in him, in you, in everybody. The world, Govinda, is not imperfect or slowly evolving along a long path to perfection. No, it is perfect at every moment; every sin already carries grace within it, all small children are potential old men, all sucklings have death within them, all dying people have eternal life. It is not possible for one person to see how far another is on the way; the Buddha exists in the robber and dice player; the robber exists in the Brahmin.

During deep meditation it is possible to dispel time, to see simultaneously all the past, present and future, and then everything is good, everything is perfect, everything is Brahman. Therefore, it seems to me that everything that exists is good—death as well as life, sin as well as holiness, wisdom as well as folly. Everything is necessary, everything needs only my agreement, my assent, my loving understanding; then all is well with me and nothing, can harm me. I learned through my body and soul that it was necessary for me to sin, that I needed lust. I learned that I had to strive for property and experience nausea and the depths of despair in order to learn not to resist them, in order to learn to love the world, and no longer compare it with some kind of desired imaginary world, some imaginary vision of perfection, but to leave it as it is, to love it and be glad to belong to it. These, Govinda, are some of the thoughts that are in my mind."

Siddhartha bent down, lifted a stone from the ground and held it in his hand.

"This," he said, handling it, "is a stone, and within a certain length of time it will perhaps be soil and from the soil it will become plant, animal or man. Previously I would have said, This stone is just a stone; it has no value, it belongs to the world of Maya, but perhaps because within the cycle of change it can also become man and spirit, it is also of importance. That is what I would have thought. But now I think, this stone is stone; it is also animal, God and Buddha. I do not respect and love it because it was one thing and will become something else, but because it has already long been everything and always is everything. I love it just because it is a stone, because today and now it appears to me a stone. I see value and meaning in each one of its fine markings and cavities, in the yellow, in the grey, in the hardness and the sound of it when I knock it, in the dryness or dampness of its surface. There are stones that feel like oil or soap, that look like leaves or sand,

and each one is different and worships Om in its own way; each one is Brahman. At the same time it is very much stone, oily or soapy, and that is just what pleases me and seems wonderful and worthy of worship. But I will say no more about it. Words do not express thoughts very well. They always become a little different immediately they are expressed; a little distorted, a little foolish. And yet it also pleases me and seems right that what is of value and wisdom to one man seems nonsense to another."

Govinda had listened in silence. "Why did you tell me about the stone?" he asked hesitatingly, after a pause.

"I did so unintentionally. But perhaps it illustrates that I just love the stone and the river and all these things that we see and from which we can learn. I can love a stone, Govinda, and a tree or a piece of bark. These are things and one can love things. But one cannot love words.

Therefore teachings are of no use to me; they have no hardness, no softness, nor colours, no corners, no smell, no taste—they have nothing but words. Perhaps that is what prevents you from finding peace; perhaps there are too many words, for even salvation and virtue. Samsara and nirvana are only words, Govinda. Nirvana is not a thing; there is only the word nirvana."

Govinda said, "Nirvana is not only a word, my friend; it is a thought."

Siddhartha continued, "It may be a thought, but I must confess, my friend, that I do not differentiate very much between thoughts and words. Quite frankly, I do not attach great importance to thoughts either. I attach more importance to things. For example, there was a man at this ferry who was my predecessor and teacher. He was a holy man who for many years believed only in the river and nothing else. He noticed that the river's voice spoke to him. He learned from it; it educated and taught him. The river seemed like a god to him and for many years he did not know that every wind, every cloud, every bird, every beetle is equally divine and knows and can teach just as well as the esteemed river. But when this holy man went off into the woods, he knew everything; he knew more than you and I, without teachers, without books, just because he believed in the river."

Govinda said, "But what you call thing, is it something real, something intrinsic? Is it not only the illusion of Maya, only image and appearance? Your stone, your tree, are they real?"

"This also does not trouble me much," said Siddhartha. "If they are illusion, then I also am illusion, and so they are always of the same nature as myself. It is that which makes them so loveable and venerable. That is why I can love them. And here is a doctrine at which you will laugh. It seems to me, Govinda, that love is the most important thing in the world. It may be important to great thinkers to examine the world, to explain and despise it. But I think it is only important to love the world, not to despise it, not for us to hate each other, but to be able to regard the world and ourselves and all beings with love, admiration and respect."

"I understand that," said Govinda, "but that is just what the Illustrious One called illusion. He preached benevolence, forbearance, sympathy, patience—but not love. He forbade us to bind ourselves to earthly love."

"I know that," said Siddhartha smiling radiantly, "I know that, Govinda, and here we find ourselves within the maze of meanings, within the conflict of words, for I will not deny that my words about love are in apparent contradiction to the teachings of Gautama. That is just why I distrust words so much, for I know that this contradiction is an illusion. I know that I am at one with Gautama. How, indeed, could he not know love, he who has recognised all humanity's vanity and transitoriness, yet loves humanity so much that he has devoted a long life solely to help and teach people? Also, with this great teacher, the thing to me is of greater importance than the words; his deeds and life are more important to me than his talk—the gesture of his hand is more important to me than his opinions. Not in speech or thought do I regard him as a great man, but in his deeds and life."

The two old men were silent for a long time. Then as Govinda was preparing to go, he said, "I thank you, Siddhartha, for telling me something of your thoughts. Some of them are strange thoughts. I cannot grasp them all immediately. However, I thank you, and I wish you many peaceful days."

Inwardly, however, he thought, Siddhartha is a strange man and he expresses strange thoughts. His ideas seem crazy. How different do the Illustrious One's doctrines sound! They are clear, straightforward, and comprehensible; they contain nothing strange, wild or laughable. But Siddhartha's hands and feet, his eyes, his brow, his breathing, his smile, his greeting, his gait affect me differently from his thoughts. Never, since the time our Illustrious Gautama passed into nirvana, have I ever met a man with the exception of Siddhartha about whom I felt, "This is a holy man!" His ideas may be strange, his words may sound foolish, but his glance and his hand, his skin and his hair, all radiate a purity, peace, serenity, gentleness and saintliness which I have never seen in any man since the recent death of our illustrious teacher.

While Govinda was thinking these thoughts and there was conflict in his heart, he again bowed to Siddhartha, full of affection towards him. He bowed low before the quietly seated man.

"Siddhartha," he said, "we are now old men. We may never see each other again in this life. I can see, my dear friend, that you have found peace. I realise that I have not found it. Tell me one more word, my esteemed friend, tell me something that I can conceive, something I can understand! Give me something to help me on my way, Siddhartha. My path is often hard and dark."

Siddhartha was silent and looked at him with his calm, peaceful smile. Govinda looked steadily into his face, with anxiety, with longing. Suffering, continual seeking and continual failure was written in his look.

Siddhartha saw it and smiled.

"Bend near to me!" he whispered in Govinda's ear. "Come, still nearer, quite close! Kiss me on the forehead, Govinda."

Although surprised, Govinda was compelled by a great love and presentiment to obey him; he leaned close to him and touched his forehead with his lips. As he did this, something wonderful happened to him. While he was still dwelling on Siddhartha's strange words, while he strove in vain to dispel the conception of time, to imagine nirvana and samsara as one, while even a certain contempt for his friend's words conflicted with a tremendous love and esteem for him, this happened to him.

He no longer saw the face of his friend Siddhartha. Instead he saw other faces, many faces, a long series, a continuous stream of faces, hundreds, thousands, which all came and disappeared and yet all seemed to be there at the same time, which all continually changed and renewed themselves and which were yet all Siddhartha. He saw the face of a fish, of a carp, with tremendous painfully opened mouth, a dying fish with dimmed eyes. He saw the face of a newly born child, red and full of wrinkles, ready to cry. He saw the face of a murderer, saw him plunge a knife into the body of a man; at the same moment he saw this criminal kneeling down, bound, and his head cut off by an executioner. He saw the naked bodies of men and women in the postures and transports of passionate love. He saw corpses stretched out, still, cold, and empty. He saw the heads of animals, boars, crocodiles, elephants, oxen, and birds. He saw Krishna and Agni. He saw all these forms and faces in a thousand relationships to each other, all helping each other, loving, hating and destroying each other and becoming newly born.

Each one was mortal, a passionate, painful example of all that is transitory. Yet none of them died; they only changed, were always reborn, continually had a new face—only time stood between one face and another. And all these forms and faces rested, flowed, reproduced, swam past and merged into each other—and over them all there was continually something thin, unreal and yet existing, stretched across like thin glass or ice, like a transparent skin, shell, form or mask of water. This

mask was Siddhartha's smiling face, which Govinda
touched with his lips at that moment.

And Govinda saw that this mask-like smile,
this smile of unity over the flowing forms, this smile
of simultaneousness over the thousands of births
and deaths, this smile of Siddhartha, was exactly
the same as the calm, delicate, impenetrable, perhaps gracious, perhaps mocking, wise, thousand-
fold smile of Gautama, the Buddha. For he had
perceived it with awe a hundred times. It was in
such a manner, Govinda knew, that the Perfect
One smiled.

No longer knowing whether time existed,
whether this display had lasted a second or a hundred years, whether there was a Siddhartha, or a
Gautama, a Self and others, wounded deeply by
a divine arrow which gave him pleasure, deeply
enchanted and exalted, Govinda stood yet awhile
bending over Siddhartha's peaceful face which
he had just kissed, which had just been the stage
of all present and future forms. His countenance
was unchanged after the mirror of the thousand-
fold forms had disappeared from the surface. He

smiled peacefully and gently, perhaps very gra-
ciously, perhaps very mockingly, exactly as the
Illustrious One had smiled.

Govinda bowed low. Uncontrollable tears
trickled down his old face. A feeling of great love,
of the most humble veneration, overwhelmed him.
He bowed low, right down to the ground, in front
of the man sitting there motionless, whose smile
reminded him of everything that he had ever loved
in his life, of everything that had ever been of value
and holy in his life.

MORE TITLES ON FICTION
FROM PILGRIMS PUBLISHING

www.pilgrimsbooks.com

For more details about Pilgrims
and other books published by them
you may visit our website at
www.pilgrimsbooks.com
or
for Mail Order and Catalogue
contact us at

Pilgrims Book House
B. 27/98 A-8 Nawab Ganj Road
Durga Kund Varanasi 221010
Tel. 91-542-2314060
Fax. 91-542-2312456
E-mail: pilgrimsbooks@sify.com

PILGRIMS BOOK HOUSE (New Delhi)
2391, Tilak Street, Chuna Mandi, Paharganj,
New Delhi 110055
Tel: (91-11) 23584015, 23584839, Fax: 23584019
E-mail: pilgrim@del2.vsnl.net.in
E-mail: pilgrimsinde@gmail.com

PILGRIMS BOOK HOUSE (Kathmandu)
P O Box 3872, Thamel, Kathmandu, Nepal
Tel: 977-1-4700942,
Off: 977-1-4700919,
Fax: 977-1-4700943
E-mail: pilgrims@wlink.com.np